"So, Aaron, have you decided who your lucky date will be for the prom?" Jessica asked point-blank. "Could it be . . . *me?*"

Aaron pretended to ponder the question. "It's not you," he replied. "I'm too *cranky* for you, remember?"

"Oh, let's put that behind us," Jessica said, forcing out a laugh. "A silly mistake. You can't imagine—"

"Excuse me," a voice behind Jessica interrupted. Jessica cringed. "Please stop harassing my prom date."

Jessica wheeled around to face Heather Mallone. *Oh, no!* Jessica thought. *Not her.* Heather was the cocaptain of the cheerleading squad along with Jessica, and she and Heather had been bitter rivals from the first day Heather had moved to town. *Anyone but her!*

Heather sat down on Aaron's lap, and he clinched his arms around her waist.

This is a nightmare, Jessica thought.

As Aaron kissed Heather's neck Jessica closed her eyes, feeling like her head was going to explode.

Shunned by the boys at Sweet Valley High. She popped open her eyes and pushed blindly through the crowd back toward the booth where Lila waited.

The world is coming to an end.

SWEET VALLEY High®

A PICTURE-PERFECT PROM?

Written by
Kate William

Created by
FRANCINE PASCAL

BANTAM BOOKS
NEW YORK • TORONTO • LONDON • SYDNEY • AUCKLAND

RL 6, age 12 and up

A PICTURE-PERFECT PROM?
A Bantam Book / June 1998

Sweet Valley High® *is a registered trademark of Francine Pascal.*
Conceived by Francine Pascal.
Produced by Daniel Weiss Associates, Inc.
33 West 17th Street
New York, NY 10011.
Cover photography by Michael Segal.

ISBN: 0-553-49231-4

Published simultaneously in the United States and Canada

Bantam Books are published by Bantam Books, a division of Bantam
Doubleday Dell Publishing Group, Inc. Its trademark, consisting of the
words "Bantam Books" and the portrayal of a rooster, is Registered in U.S.
Patent and Trademark Office and in other countries. Marca Registrada.
Bantam Books, 1540 Broadway, New York, New York 10036.

PRINTED IN THE UNITED STATES OF AMERICA

OPM   0 9 8 7 6 5 4 3 2 1

To Lara Fischer-Zernin

Chapter 1

"Bibi's just got in an amazing new collection of prom dresses," sixteen-year-old Jessica Wakefield told her best friend, Lila Fowler. Bibi's was an incredibly trendy dress boutique in the Valley Mall. "*Très* fab."

Lila sniffed as she stepped into the Sweet Valley High parking lot. "Who did you hear *that* from?" she asked disdainfully, tossing her long brown hair. "I can't believe Bibi managed to pull a new line together so quickly. Just last week her collection was, oh . . . *très drab*."

Jessica giggled. The prom was only a few weeks away, and she and Lila were heading over to the mall to get started on acquiring the most important part of any prom—the perfect dress. Ever since the final bell of the school day had rung, Jessica and Lila had been carefully planning their attack on the stores in order to get the best dresses possible. But so far they hadn't been able to agree on where to start their shopping invasion.

"Oh, I think Sandy mentioned stopping in at Bibi's yesterday," Jessica replied. Sandy Bacon used to be a member of Jessica's cheerleading squad and was a friend of both Jessica and Lila.

"You're going to trust *Sandy?*" Lila asked as she carefully made her way between the cars in the lot. "Don't get me wrong, Sandy's a doll, but the girl's taste is definitely . . . suspect."

"Agreed," Jessica said. "Did you see the red, white, and blue jumper she was wearing today?"

"Painful," Lila murmured, shaking her head sorrowfully.

"But I love her to death," Jessica pointed out quickly.

"Oh, no question," Lila replied.

"So, fine, we don't start at Bibi's. Where, then? Lisette's?"

Lila stopped short in the middle of the parking lot, and Jessica almost bumped into her. "Jessica," Lila said, turning slowly in a circle to look around. "Where'd you park your Jeep? You always park right here. But I don't see it."

Jessica peered over the cars surrounding her, searching for any sign of the black Jeep Wrangler she shared with her twin sister. "That's funny," she muttered. "Liz wouldn't have taken it. . . ." She gasped and pressed her hand to her forehead. "Duh!" she exclaimed, shaking her head. "We took our mother's wagon today. The Jeep—poor thing—is in the shop. Somehow Wilkins managed to drive it over a cliff after he asked Liz to marry him."

"How dramatic," Lila said. "So, where's the station wagon?"

Jessica pointed to the far end of the lot. "I parked it in the corner so nobody would see us driving something so lame," she replied. "But Liz has the keys."

Lila sighed. "You're exhausting me, Jessica, and we haven't even started shopping yet."

Jessica grinned and grabbed her best friend's hand, dragging her back toward the school. "Liz is probably in the *Oracle* office as usual," she said. "C'mon, it'll only take a second. Then we'll hit Lisette's."

"Jessica, do not *pull* me," Lila protested, but she followed along. "And Lisette's? Why there? That place is *so* early eighties."

For some reason Jessica had a sudden strong, positive feeling about that particular boutique. Her fingers tingled—a sure sign she was on the right track. But how to convince Lila to start at Lisette's? There was only one way to persuade the snobbiest and richest girl at Sweet Valley High. "It's very expensive," Jessica commented.

"You're right," Lila said. "We'll start at Lisette's."

A few minutes later Jessica burst into the *Oracle* office. "Liz!" she cried. "I need Mom's keys!"

Jessica's identical twin sister, Elizabeth, looked up from where she had been hunched over a big drafting table beside Penny Ayala, the editor in chief of the school newspaper, and Olivia Davidson, the arts editor. Both Olivia and Penny groaned as they saw Jessica and Lila enter. Jessica rolled her eyes at them. She didn't really care if Elizabeth's nerdy friends liked her or not.

Olivia was simply weird, with her funky, sometimes homemade outfits and wild tangles of dark hair. Jessica knew Olivia was a talented artist, but the girl was too oddball for Jessica's taste. Penny, on the other hand, was tall and lanky, with short brown hair. And she was totally uptight. She was always insanely driven about her journalism career. Jessica couldn't understand why Elizabeth hung around them so much.

But then, their choice of friends was only one of the many differences between Jessica and Elizabeth Wakefield. In spite of their absolutely identical sun-kissed shoulder-length blond hair, willowy athletic figures, and bright eyes the color of the Pacific Ocean, their interests and personalities were as different as sweater sets and ball gowns. Jessica lived for the moment, always seeking out wild adventures to keep her busy, always scheming new ways to thrust herself into the limelight. She dressed to impress. Someday, Jessica knew, she was going to be a famous model or movie star. In the meantime she kept herself active hanging out with her friends, going to parties, chatting about guys, and being the cocaptain of the Sweet Valley High cheerleading squad. And dating a continual progression of incredibly cute guys, of course.

Elizabeth, the older twin by four minutes, was a lot more reserved. She preferred to stay behind the scenes, writing articles for the *Oracle*, concentrating on schoolwork, and going to movies or having coffee with her best friends, Maria Slater and Enid Rollins. Elizabeth dressed conservatively and comfortably. Her goal in life was to be a professional writer someday. *Either that,* Jessica thought with a chuckle, *or a senator—someone powerful, dependable, and . . . bossy.* Elizabeth usually only dated one guy, her dull, longtime boyfriend Todd Wilkins, but lately her romantic life had been in major upheaval.

"Jess," Elizabeth replied calmly, "we discussed this already. We decided I could have Mom's car this afternoon. I need to go to the prom committee meeting after I finish helping Penny."

"C'mon, Liz," Jessica wheedled. "It's an emergency."

Elizabeth narrowed her eyes suspiciously. "What emergency?"

Jessica decided to change the subject, knowing that her twin didn't share her concern over buying the perfect prom dress. She peered at the black-and-white layout on the drafting table. It looked pretty boring, but maybe she was mentioned in it. "What's this?" she asked.

Nobody replied—in fact, the girls on the *Oracle* staff seemed pretty uncomfortable—so Jessica quickly scanned it. Her eyes widened as she read. Jessica wasn't mentioned in it—always a disappointment—but she saw that it was an advertisement. For a prom date!

"Jessica," Lila whined. "Hurry up. I just shivered, so someone is probably touching the prom dress meant for me. We've got to get there before someone buys it!"

"Your emergency is shopping?" Elizabeth asked, raising an eyebrow.

Jessica ignored her twin for the moment. "Who's desperate enough to actually *advertise* for a prom date?" she asked with a laugh.

Penny cleared her throat. "I am," she replied, with only a tiny trace of embarrassment in her voice. "And it's not desperation. It's practicality."

"Whatever," Lila whispered in Jessica's ear. "Sounds like desperation to me."

"Doesn't it make you feel . . . oh, I don't know—like a used sewing machine?" Jessica asked Penny. "And what about Neil?" Neil Freemount was Penny's boyfriend.

"Jess!" Elizabeth scolded.

Penny shook her head. "It's OK," she said. "I'm fine with it, Jessica. Neil has a great internship in Chicago this summer, but it starts early and he's

6

going to miss the dance. But just because my boyfriend can't make it shouldn't mean I have to skip my own senior prom! I want to be there with all my friends, and I should be there to cover it for the *Oracle*."

Jessica smirked—Penny sounded a little overdefensive.

"I've decided to treat the prom almost as a professional necessity rather than a romantic event," Penny continued. "So I have to find a date with no emotional involvement. It's that simple."

Jessica spotted Elizabeth's backpack, unzipped the front pocket, and starting fishing around for the keys to the station wagon. "Sounds kind of sad to me," she told Penny.

"I think it's brave . . . and independent," Olivia said.

"Nope," Lila murmured. "Sad. Like renting a prom dress instead of buying one." She shuddered.

Elizabeth turned to Jessica, her eyes blazing. "Who are *you* going with, Jess?" she asked pointedly. "How about you, Lila? People without dates shouldn't be so quick to judge."

Jessica froze as her hand closed over the keys to their mother's station wagon. Elizabeth was absolutely right—Jessica didn't have a prom date . . . and neither did Lila. Yet. She relaxed and pulled the keys out of Elizabeth's backpack. Like finding a date was going to be a problem for them! She'd often had to juggle two dates in one weekend! She glanced over at Lila, and when she saw the amusement twinkling in her best friend's brown eyes, Jessica couldn't help laughing hard and loud at the very idea that the two most popular—and beautiful—girls in Sweet Valley wouldn't be able to find dates for the prom.

Lila let out a dainty snort of laughter. "Preposterous," she muttered.

Jessica composed herself. "Get real, Liz," she told her twin. "Finding a date is not the issue. Guys will be knocking down our doors. *Not* a problem." She jangled the keys in front of Elizabeth's face. "Besides, big sister, have you asked yourself the same question?"

Elizabeth's mouth dropped open, and her eyes filled with pain. "That's not fair, Jess," she whispered. Jessica immediately felt guilty for broaching the subject of her twin's troubled romantic life. Elizabeth had recently been dating both Todd Wilkins and Devon Whitelaw, a gorgeous newcomer to Sweet Valley. After Devon and Todd had gotten into a huge fight—which almost led to Todd's death in a terrible accident—Elizabeth had decided she needed space to figure out how she felt. And she'd broken up with them both, even though Todd had given her a ring and asked Elizabeth to marry him! Jessica knew that Elizabeth would be heartsick over her decision for a long time to come. She just couldn't bounce back from romantic disaster as fast as Jessica could.

8

Jessica sighed. "I'm sorry, Lizzie," she said. "You know I didn't mean it. It just popped out. I'm just overexcited about shopping for my prom dress. You know Todd will come to his senses eventually." Jessica didn't mention Devon on purpose. She'd made a play for Devon early on, but he'd only had eyes for Elizabeth. Jessica might bounce back from romantic messes quicker than her twin, but it wasn't instantaneous!

"Of *course* he will, Liz," Jessica continued reassuringly. "He's forgiven you—and you've forgiven him—so many times it makes me sick. Why should this time be any different?"

"Precisely," Lila agreed.

"I've been telling you that all week," Olivia added. "Listen to your wacky sister."

A ghost of a smile played on Elizabeth's lips. "I guess you're right," she said.

"I'm always right." Jessica cleared her throat. "So, you don't mind if I take Mom's car?"

Now Elizabeth smiled for real. "Oh, I guess not. I can always get a ride to the committee meeting from Enid."

Jessica leaned down and planted a quick kiss on Elizabeth's cheek. "Great!" she exclaimed. "Liz, you're the best. We're outta here." She was already turning and heading for the door.

"Toodles," Lila said with a wave as she followed Jessica.

Once they had made it out into the hallway,

Jessica turned to Lila, shaking the keys triumphantly. "Lisette's?" she breathed.

"Definitely," Lila confirmed.

"Do you have any ideas for the prom theme?" Enid Rollins asked Elizabeth. They were in Enid's car, heading over to the prom committee meeting at Winston Egbert's house. "I can't think of a single one."

Elizabeth shifted in the passenger seat. "Not yet," she admitted. "I've got a few ideas, but they're still pretty vague." She didn't really feel like discussing the design theme for the prom. All afternoon Elizabeth had been brooding over her messy love life. Her turbulent feelings made concentrating on planning the prom difficult . . . and a little painful.

"You OK, Liz?" Enid asked. "You've been pretty quiet since we left school."

Elizabeth smiled at her best friend. Jessica always wondered why Elizabeth hung around with Enid, whom Jessica considered too shy, studious, and socially awkward to be any fun. But Elizabeth knew that there was nobody warmer or more supportive than the girl with reddish brown curly hair sitting beside her. Enid might be a little shy, but once she warmed up, there was no one more loyal on earth. *She always knows when I'm confused,* Elizabeth thought. *And she's the best listener I know. But I don't feel like talking about it right now.*

"I'm fine," Elizabeth said. "Just a little pre-occupied today."

"OK," Enid said amicably. "Back to the prom theme. What do you think if we—"

"Do you think Todd's going to be at the meeting?" Elizabeth interrupted. She blushed furiously. She hadn't meant to blurt that out at all, but lately her confused emotions were right near the surface—and always ready to burst through.

Enid chuckled. "You have Todd on the brain, huh? I thought so."

Elizabeth shook her head ruefully. "I can't stop thinking about him and Devon," she confessed. "My life's such a wreck, the president should declare it an official disaster area."

"Hmmm. I don't think it's as bad as *you* think it is," Enid said carefully. "*You* made the decision to break up with both of them. I say, good. That's not a mess, that's taking control of your life, figuring out what *you* really want. Todd and Devon were tearing you in two, and you were just going to end up hurting all three of you. This way you get to make your decision calmly."

Elizabeth sighed. "You're right," she admitted. "But I can't help wondering what Todd's been up to. I haven't even said more than two words to him since he got out of the hospital. I'm just so used to knowing about his life that . . . I feel like I'm in withdrawal. Have you heard . . ." Elizabeth let her voice trail away, not wanting to finish her sentence.

11

"What?" Enid prompted. "Have I heard what?"

A hot blush crept over Elizabeth's face. "Have you heard if Todd's seeing anyone else?"

Enid laughed. "Get real, Liz," she said. "This is Todd we're talking about. He'll be devoted to you until the day he dies. He asked you to marry him just a few weeks ago! And Devon's crazy about you. The two of them are probably just waiting around for you to make a decision."

"You know," Elizabeth replied thoughtfully. "In my stronger moments I think ditching them both so I have time to think is the best thing I could've done."

"It is," Enid agreed.

"In fact, I feel pretty good about the whole thing," Elizabeth concluded in a determined voice, mostly believing it. *Of course*, she thought, *if I'm totally honest with myself, the fact that I've been avoiding both Todd and Devon like the plague might have something to do with whatever sense of well-being I have.*

"Good for you," Enid said. She steered the car around a sharp curve and headed down the long block toward Winston's house.

Elizabeth groaned. "I wish I could just be friends with them both. That would solve everything."

"OK," Enid said with a shrug. "Sounds good to me."

"Oh, who am I kidding?" Elizabeth exclaimed.

12

"I'm completely in love with both of them. Friendship—*just* friendship—would be absolutely impossible."

"When you're right, you're right," Enid said evenly.

They both laughed. Elizabeth lightly poked her best friend on the arm. "You know," she said in an amused voice, "there's such a thing as being *too* supportive. You can't take both sides!"

"Sure, I can," Enid replied. "When both sides are right." She pulled into Winston's driveway, parked behind Maria Santelli's car, and killed the engine. "So, what are you going to do if Todd's here? There's a very good chance he will be, you know."

Elizabeth clenched her jaw. "I'll hang out with him," she answered. "I'll make a point of it. After all, I still care about Todd—and talking to him will make it easier for us to get used to being friends, get over whatever awkwardness is left. All it takes is time . . . and exposure. It'll be fine."

"That's the spirit," Enid said. She opened the car door. "Ready?"

Elizabeth unbuckled her seat belt. "Ready," she replied firmly.

Winston answered the door only seconds after Enid knocked. He was balancing a giant bowl of tortilla chips on one arm, with liter bottles of soda dangling between his fingers. Winston looked even more awkward and gangly than usual as he

13

struggled with the food and the door. "Hurry!" he called. "Help me! I'm dropping these!"

Enid rescued the bowl of chips, and Elizabeth grabbed two bottles of soda. "Honestly, Win, why didn't you put the bowl down before opening the door?" Enid asked.

Winston smiled his goofy grin. "Didn't think of it," he explained. "C'mon in, we're all down in the rec room."

The Egberts' rec room was really a barely converted basement. The floor was bare concrete, and a giant boiler lurked in the corner, but in spite of its unfinished state it felt rather homey. An entire wall was covered with overflowing bookshelves, and Mrs. Egbert had put up rich blue curtains over the high basement windows. In the center of the large room card tables were set up, surrounded by odd old furniture—a long white vinyl couch, butterfly chairs, metal folding chairs, and a big battered recliner that had been scratched up by cats. As Elizabeth set the drinks down on the card table she smiled at Olivia, standing behind the couch with her new boyfriend, Ken Matthews, the captain of the football team. On the other side of the room were Deedee Gordon and Maria Santelli, Winston's girlfriend. Behind Maria, Elizabeth saw Aaron Dallas talking to Tad "Blubber" Johnson, and . . .

Elizabeth gulped. *Todd.* He was facing away from her, and she focused intently on him as he laughed at something Aaron said. For a second she closed her eyes, the sound of his warm laughter floating in her mind. He looked wonderful, with his tall basketball player's build, his broad shoulders, and his wavy dark brown hair that she longed to run her fingers through. Elizabeth knew she was staring, and she told herself to turn away before he—

Too late, she thought as he suddenly turned around, as though sensing she was there. All traces of his laughter fell away as he spotted her. His deep coffee-colored eyes filled with pain and longing, and he lowered his head, obviously hurt by the simple sight of her.

Elizabeth's stomach flip-flopped, and her mouth went dry. *Why did I ever think we could just be friends?* she berated herself harshly. *Was I out of my mind?*

She turned to find Enid standing beside her, eating a chip. Enid's face looked startled as she saw Elizabeth's expression. "What's wrong?" Enid asked.

Instead of replying Elizabeth grabbed Enid's hand and dragged her over to the other side of the room, heading for Olivia and Ken.

As far away from Todd as possible.

Chapter 2

Devon Whitelaw stepped out of The Breakfast Nook, a trendy kitchen furnishings shop in the Valley Mall. He'd just bought a kitchen rack for his guardian, Nan Johnstone. *It's perfect,* he thought as he tucked the box underneath his arm. *It'll save her from bending over all the time to get the pots in that low cabinet.*

Devon adjusted the collar of his soft brown leather jacket as he joined the crowds milling in the busy corridors of the mall. He smiled, picturing the expression on Nan's face when he presented the rack to her. She would probably look dismayed at first, her creased brow wrinkling up in a frown of disapproval. "Devon, you shouldn't have," she'd say, or, "So I bend over a little; what's the big deal?" But Devon knew she'd be secretly pleased. And he was surprised at how good he felt about spending his money giving his old nanny gifts, especially since he knew she'd never ask.

Which was exactly why he loved doing things for her. Because Nan Johnstone was the only person in the world who didn't expect anything from him, who loved him for him. And in return he trusted her completely . . . and shared his huge inheritance with her in spite of her wishes.

Why is it, he wondered philosophically as he turned a corner in the mall, *that we only really enjoy doing what isn't required of us?*

Devon stopped short, faced with a gaudy prom display in a boutique. His lip curled in distaste as he stared at the long flowing gowns and cheesy tuxedos on the mannequins in the window.

Proms are so stupid, he thought. *A perfect example of my theory. The prom is this big requirement, where you're a loser if you don't go. Don't miss out on the biggest event of your life!* He snorted in derision. *The excitement is so . . . manufactured.*

Devon sighed loudly and shifted the box under his arm to a more comfortable position. *What's the point of the prom anyway?* he wondered. *If everybody wants to dance and get together, why not have a party somewhere? Why make such a big deal out of it?*

Nobody at Sweet Valley High had been able to talk about anything else lately—who's going with whom, where to get the best tuxedo, how to match corsages—endlessly, on and on and on. Devon was completely sick of hearing about the prom. He clenched his fists. *It's just an excuse to spend a lot of money trying to outdo everyone else,* he thought hotly.

Of course, since he'd inherited his parents' fortune, he could put everyone else in school to shame. He had great style and the money to back it up, but what was the point? What would it prove? Devon wouldn't go to the prom even if someone paid *him.*

He frowned, still staring at the overdressed mannequins in the shop window. *Unless . . . ,* he admitted to himself, *unless Elizabeth wanted to go with me. . . .*

Devon shook his head violently, trying to clear his thoughts. *Stupid,* he told himself harshly. *Don't be stupid. Elizabeth wants nothing to do with you, and you know it.*

But as he forced himself to turn away from the shop window he caught a glimpse of a golden blond reflection in the plate glass.

His heart skipped a beat. Adrenaline surging through his veins, Devon whirled around to check out the source of the reflection. *Elizabeth!* he thought wildly. *She's here!* It was as though simply thinking her name had somehow conjured her up from thin air.

And there she was, just coming around the corner, looking away from him. He swallowed nervously as he stepped forward to intercept her. Nobody else on earth had this effect on him. Nobody. Devon loved Elizabeth Wakefield with his heart, body, and soul.

But in his rush to reach her, Devon noticed Lila Fowler following Elizabeth around the corner, hurrying to keep up. He froze in his tracks. Elizabeth—hanging out with a snob like Lila? Shopping with her? That seemed unlikely at best.

So it wasn't Elizabeth. It was Jessica.

Devon glowered at Jessica for a moment, furious with himself about getting so worked up. *They may look exactly the same, but they're entirely different where it counts,* he thought. *They're both beautiful, sure, but . . .*

But he loved Elizabeth. And Jessica was . . . not his type. Devon had been a little intrigued when Jessica had first come on to him, but there wasn't any chemistry between them. He wasn't quite certain why she irritated him so badly—maybe it was because she shared the same looks as Elizabeth. But unlike Elizabeth, who barely seemed to know she was beautiful, Jessica seemed to *use* her beauty like a weapon to get what she wanted. And Devon didn't respect that at all. He definitely didn't want to have to talk to Jessica Wakefield.

Hoping that Jessica and Lila hadn't caught sight of him, Devon quickly ducked into the prom boutique. As he strode deeper into the store he heard a little bell tinkle, which meant the door had closed behind him. Ignoring the curious stares of the shopkeeper, he slumped against a wall beside a rack of dresses, sighing with relief. He was safe.

The little doorbell tinkled again, and Devon glanced up. *Of course,* he thought.

Jessica and Lila sauntered into the store, chattering to each other.

Might as well get this over with. Devon stood up straight and faced them.

Jessica saw him immediately. Her face lit up in a wide, dazzling smile as she hurried over. "Devon!" she called excitedly. "Hi!"

Devon forced himself to return her smile, bracing himself for the worst. When they'd first met, Jessica had come on to him strong. And although he'd proved that he didn't return her affections, she was acting perfectly friendly at the moment, and he didn't trust her motives. "Hello," he said evenly.

"What are you doing in here?" Jessica asked. "Getting a tux?"

"Jessica," Lila complained, coming up behind her. "Don't rush everywhere. You know I can't run in these shoes." Then Lila seemed to notice Devon's presence. "Oh, hello, Devon," Lila told him coolly.

"Nah," Devon replied to Jessica's question. "I'm just . . . browsing, I guess."

"Really?" Jessica breathed, as though he'd just said something meaningful and witty. She stared into his eyes, a smirk playing on her lips, obviously flirting. "You're certainly looking well."

"Thanks," Devon told her flatly. He didn't want to look away from Jessica's gaze because he didn't want her to think she had an effect on him, but the intensity of her stare was unnerving. She certainly was a powerful presence—Jessica was flirty and ditzy, yes, but Devon knew a lot of that was an act, masking her downright dangerous manipulative cunning. But he could play that game too—and maybe find out something he wanted to know. "So . . . ," he said, "how's Liz?"

Devon had to stifle a smile at Jessica's reaction. She hadn't liked his question one bit—her eyes blazed with anger. But she controlled herself quickly. "Oh," she replied with forced lightness, "she's just fine. I haven't seen her all that much, though. She's been so busy with the prom committee and everything. In fact, she's at a meeting right now . . . probably rubbing shoulders with . . . Todd."

Now it was Devon's turn to flinch. Jessica had scored a serious point. He could already feel his fury rising at the simple suggestion that Elizabeth and Todd might be in the same room somewhere. He had to get away from her before she did real damage.

He ignored Jessica's flinty smile. As icily as he could, Devon said, "Well, thanks for letting me know." Then without another word he abruptly pushed between Jessica and Lila so that they had to step aside. He headed for the door.

"Rude!" Lila called behind him.

As soon as Devon was down the corridor away from the shop he found a bench and collapsed onto it, holding his head in his hands. *Great,* he thought, *that's just great.* He couldn't get the image of Elizabeth and Todd working together side by side out of his mind. He could see their heads leaning toward each other as they discussed some tiny detail of the prom . . . the lovely furrow of her brow that Elizabeth got when she was concentrating. . . .

He tried to fight the overwhelming images and the horrible emotions surfacing with them. But he couldn't help a cold, wet blanket of jealousy from covering him.

Devon groaned. Now he really had a good reason to hate this prom thing.

In his subgroup at the committee meeting Todd was trying to listen to Maria Santelli discuss possible choices for the prom's menu. But he couldn't keep his gaze from wandering over to the other side of the rec room, where Elizabeth was laughing and joking with Winston and Enid in the theme subgroup.

"Chicken . . . or fish?" Maria asked the group as she tucked a strand of her long brown hair behind her ear. "I think chicken is probably safer. But fish is . . . more adult somehow. Any thoughts?"

Todd didn't have an opinion on fish one way or

the other. He strained to hear what Elizabeth was saying across the room, but he couldn't make out any of her words.

"There are lots of good chicken dishes," Blubber Johnson added. "I've seen in fancy restaurants where it's folded over and stuffed with bacon and covered in like a cream sauce."

"That might be . . . a little rich for us," Maria replied diplomatically. "We don't want anyone bursting out of their prom dresses."

Todd stared as Elizabeth leaned forward, obviously struck with an idea. He longed to hear what it was, to listen as she became excited over her own creativity. There was nothing so attractive to Todd in the world as Elizabeth when she got caught up in her own enthusiasm.

"What do you think, Todd?" Maria asked.

Todd sat up straight. "Uh . . . ," he said. "About what?"

Blubber and Maria laughed. "Grilled chicken," Maria replied.

"Grilled chicken is cool," Todd told her. "Sounds good to me."

As Maria started talking again Todd drifted off. Planning the menu wasn't really his thing. Usually he'd let the others do all the creative planning and then show up on the night of the prom to help set up. *I'm more of an action guy,* Todd decided.

But he had known Elizabeth would be here today. And he'd thought that if they were working together on something involving lots of school spirit, surrounded by their friends, Elizabeth would remember how much a part of her life at Sweet Valley High Todd had always been. And then she'd regret pushing him away.

It wasn't turning out that way. Todd hadn't managed to say two words to her all night—and she'd barely looked in his direction when she first showed up. And now they weren't even working together! He was wasting his time.

"Todd, what's your opinion?" Maria asked.

Todd stood up. "I'm sorry," he said. "I don't mean to be rude, but . . . I'm changing groups. I'm going to go join . . . uh . . . *Winston* and the others. No offense, OK?"

Blubber and Maria glanced at each other. Todd felt a little awkward—they obviously knew the real reason he wanted to change groups. But what they thought wasn't important. The only important thing was that he be with Elizabeth.

"Sure, Todd," Maria said pleasantly. "Go on. And good luck."

"Thanks," Todd replied. He hurried over to the theme group and stood behind Winston until their conversation paused.

"Mind if I join you?" Todd asked.

"I don't see why not," Enid replied. "Have a seat."

Todd glanced at Elizabeth. She met his eyes, and a surge of hope shot through him. She graced him with a small smile as he sat next to Winston.

"Hey, Toddy," Winston said, "tell me what you think of my June Bug theme." He cracked a wide grin. "We all dress up like insects, right? Then we drink really sweet punch that tastes kind of like bug juice. We could decorate the ballroom like a big hive. And we can even do the jitterbug!"

"I've got a better one," Todd shot back, laughing at Winston's ridiculous suggestion. "We pretend like we're marooned on a tiny island, and we wear ripped and wet clothes. We could have coconut drinks, and all the music comes from a little old radio. We could pour sand all over the ballroom . . . and put a giant palm tree in the middle of the dance floor. I call it Shipwrecked. It will be very romantic."

Enid, Winston, and Elizabeth laughed. The musical sound of Elizabeth's laughter sent a bolt of happiness right through Todd.

"Those are the worst ideas I've ever heard," Elizabeth told them, her eyes still dancing with amusement. "Todd, don't you have any real ideas?"

Todd looked down at his sneakers, thinking seriously. He wanted desperately to impress her. His suggestion had to be exactly right. And after they had dated for so long, he thought he knew what she considered truly romantic.

"Um," he began in a quiet voice. "I guess it should be . . . elegant. Like a dance from . . . oh, the 1940s. Antique tuxedos and dresses. You know, old—"

26

"Old-fashioned," Elizabeth interrupted excitedly. "Exactly," she told him warmly. "That was my suggestion exactly."

Todd smiled. And Elizabeth smiled back. Inwardly he sighed with relief. Maybe his plan to join the prom committee had been a good idea after all!

The phone rang as Jessica was applying a layer of silvery blue nail polish to her toenails. She quickly capped the bottle of polish and grabbed the phone off the floor.

"Hey," she answered cheerfully. "Wakefields'!"

"Hi, Jess," Amy Sutton said. "What's up? I just called to see how your shopping trip went today."

Amy was a pretty blond girl who was on the cheerleading squad with Jessica—and was her best friend after Lila. "Amazingly," Jessica breathed into the phone. She glanced around her bedroom, where her new purchases were strewn over the floor on top of all the other junk—CDs, shoes, schoolbooks, and clothing—*already* on the floor. "I didn't get a dress yet," she admitted. "But I saw a bunch of possibilities. And I got all the accessories. Like—"

"Did I tell you what Barry's planning for the big night?" Amy interrupted. Barry Rork was Amy's on-again, off-again boyfriend. Apparently they were on again. "He's going to take me to Chez Sam before the prom, and he's going to get the biggest corsage I've ever even heard of." Chez Sam was an extremely expensive restaurant up the coast from Sweet Valley.

"That's cool," Jessica said. "Listen, you should see the clip I bought for my hair. It's got sprigs of baby's breath attached to this comb, and—"

"Barry's being incredibly romantic," Amy broke in again. "He took an extra shift giving tennis lessons just to pay for the prom."

"That's beautiful," Jessica replied, with more than a touch of sarcasm in her voice. She flipped onto her back on her bed. "But Amy, I was explaining about my hair clip. . . . It'll go with any dress I get. And you should have seen these two dresses I saw in Lisette's—"

"And you know what else Barry did?" Amy interrupted again. Her voice grew dreamy. "He sent me a personally engraved invitation requesting the honor of my presence at the prom. Couldn't you die?"

Jessica grit her teeth in annoyance. *Blah, blah, blah, Barry,* she thought. And she *hated* being interrupted. "That's cool, Amy," Jessica allowed, sitting up on the edge of her bed. "But let me tell you about this dress I saw. It's snow-white, with the most daring scooped neckline—"

"It's going to be the most wonderful night of my life," Amy broke in again. "Barry—"

"Hello!" Jessica cried into the phone. "Can you stop talking about Barry for a second, please?

28

We're discussing something important here—what we're going to wear."

Amy sniffed, sounding hurt. "I didn't mean to bore you, Jess," Amy said huffily. "I was just excited, that's all. I don't think it's too strange for me to be excited over my prom date." Amy paused for a second. "Have *you* found a date yet, Jessica?" she asked pointedly.

"No," Jessica replied calmly. "But I'm not worried in the least. I haven't decided who the lucky guy will be, but you know he'll be the hottest date there."

"You'd better decide soon," Amy warned. "The prom is only a few weeks away, you know."

Jessica laughed. "Whatever, Aim. There are more important things to worry about—like limos. Has Barry hired one yet?" she asked.

"I don't think so," Amy replied.

"Well," Jessica said smoothly, "I know the exact kind I want. . . ."

Chapter 3

Elizabeth leaned across the lunch table toward Maria Slater and Enid in the school cafeteria the next day. "It's such a relief," she admitted in a hushed voice. "When Todd said he wanted the prom to be elegant and old-fashioned too, I just knew we were on the same page again. We were talking just like we used to. I'm so glad the ice between us is melting. Finally."

"That's wonderful, Liz," Enid said sincerely. "So are you going to start dating him again?"

Elizabeth felt a little shocked. That certainly wasn't what she meant! "No, no," she protested. "I still think taking time off from Todd and Devon was the best thing I could've done. I'm just glad I'm getting to be friends with Todd again. That's all."

"Just friends, huh?" Maria asked with a smile,

her dark eyes flashing with amusement.

Elizabeth hadn't been best friends with Maria all that long—only since the tall, striking former child actress with flawless ebony skin had moved back to Sweet Valley from New York. But Elizabeth valued Maria's down-to-earth, witty wisdom as much as she treasured Enid's thoughtful sensitivity. Right now, though, Maria obviously didn't believe a word Elizabeth was saying.

Elizabeth smirked at her. "Yes," she said firmly. "Just friends. Now if I could only do the same thing with Devon." She sighed loudly. "But that seems impossible."

"With that boy," Maria told her, "*you've* got to make the first move. He's the most reserved guy I've ever met. And now that you've hurt him— sorry, but you did—he's never going to come out of his shell."

"I know." Elizabeth sighed again. "You're right, you're right. But what's the move?"

"Ask him to the prom," Maria replied. She grinned wickedly.

"Maria!" Elizabeth scolded over Enid's laughter. "Get real."

"I'm not joking," Maria continued. "Well, maybe only half joking. I mean, Liz, have you decided which one you're going to take yet?"

A funny, sick feeling settled in Elizabeth's stomach. "I've gone back and forth over it," she confessed to her friends. "And I've reached a decision."

"What?" Enīd asked.

"That it's ridiculous to consider," Elizabeth replied. "I told them both that I wanted space, and they're respecting that. Neither of them is dying to go to the prom with me, I'm sure."

Enid chuckled. "Well, Todd certainly didn't seem to be respecting your space at the meeting yesterday," she told Elizabeth. "In fact, he looked like a guy desperate to get his girlfriend back before the prom."

"You think so?" Elizabeth asked softly. Then she shook her head. "No. No way. He was only being friendly, I'm sure of it."

"Uh-huh," Maria said sarcastically. "Right."

"It's true!" Elizabeth protested. "It's stupid to assume that Todd and Devon are just waiting around for me to pick one of them—they have lives too, you know."

Maria and Enid glanced at each other and then cracked up. "Todd," Maria gasped, "having a life outside you? And just what would that be . . . besides basketball, I mean?"

Elizabeth had to chuckle. "Stop," she said. "Don't be mean. And anyway, I'm not sure who I'd want to go with even if the decision was mine to make." *Although,* she admitted to herself, *joking around with Todd was fun last night. . . .* "I'm just going to wait until one of them asks me. And if they don't, then they don't. It's as simple as that."

"It's never that simple," Maria countered.

Right at that moment Elizabeth caught sight of a tall, gorgeous guy passing their table. He had dark brown hair sculpted into a perfect flip; red, sensuous lips; a trim, muscular body; and he walked like a panther—as though every step used only the barest fraction of the coiled energy within him. . . . *Devon,* she realized, her heart hammering in her chest. She sat up straight, unable to stop herself from staring at him.

Devon returned her stare until Elizabeth felt a warm rush of emotion crash over her from the intensity of his gaze. She attempted a tentative smile.

He immediately turned away and strode out of the cafeteria.

Elizabeth pressed her hand to her hot forehead. She would never get used to the wild, bewildering effect Devon had on her. Now she felt more confused than ever.

Enid sighed, interrupting Elizabeth's trance. "Liz, I wish I had your problem," she said sadly. "I'd kill to have two hot guys fighting over me. I have a feeling nobody's going to ask me to the prom at all."

Elizabeth shook her head to clear the leftover confusion of seeing Devon. She put her hand on Enid's arm. "That's not true," she said.

"*So* not true," Maria added loyally. "You just wait and see."

The final bell of the day rang, breaking into Devon's churning thoughts. He absentmindedly began pushing his books together, unable to stop staring blankly at the wall.

Why didn't I stop to talk to her at lunchtime? he berated himself. *What's wrong with me?* It was all he wanted to do—to go sit beside Elizabeth and start talking, enjoying the incredible connection he knew they shared. But he just couldn't. Elizabeth had told him she wanted her space, and he had to respect that. Even if for the rest of the day after he saw her, it ripped out his heart.

I've got to let her make the first move, he thought. *It's only right.*

He swiped his hair off his forehead with a groan. Then he stood up and grabbed his books, still lost in thought as he headed out of the class-room.

When girls say they want space, do they mean it? he wondered as he ambled down the hall. *Or do they really want you to be all romantic and go after them anyway because you love them too much to keep away? Is Elizabeth just messing with my head? Is this a plan of hers, to push me away so that I'll want even more to be with her? Does she expect me to make the first move? Or would she freak out if she thinks I'm, like, stalking her?*

Devon's mind was spinning with so many ques-tions that he almost ran right into a group of three girls who cut suddenly across the hall. They laughed and barely noticed him as they continued on their way. Devon glared at their backs for a long moment until the girls ducked into the home economics classroom. There was a sign on the door that read Prom Committee Meeting, 2:45.

Of course, the prom, Devon thought angrily. He couldn't believe how seriously so many of the students were taking the whole prom thing—seriously enough to stay after school to plan it. *Don't they have lives?* he asked himself with a sneer. *Can't they see how superficial the prom is?*

Devon was just about to turn and head out of the school when Elizabeth came around the corner. His stomach lurched. Devon took a step toward her and then stopped, seeing for the first time that Wilkins was beside her, and she was talking earnestly to him. Devon's shoulders tensed as he saw how involved in conversation they were. Then Elizabeth laughed at something Todd said, and a dagger twisted in Devon's guts.

She's probably going to the prom with Wilkins, he realized with a sharp intake of breath.

And why not? From all the reports Devon had heard, Todd and Elizabeth had been Sweet Valley High's "perfect couple" before he had stepped in and stirred things up. It only made sense that they'd go to the prom after being in love all year.

But where did that leave Devon? *Dangling in the wind,* he thought. *Alone.*

An inferno of anger suddenly blazed up within him. He spun around and marched down the hall away from them, seeding. *Forget her,* he thought.

Forget you ever loved her. Forget the whole thing. Let Liz have her fun. Let her go on with her friends like you never even existed!

Devon wrenched open the front door of Sweet Valley High and slammed it behind him. The slam echoed in the air like the bars of a jail cell sliding into place, locking him away from the girl he loved. *Forever.*

Chapter 4

In the home ec room Enid Rollins chewed on the end of her pencil as she listened to Olivia Davidson's plan for the design subgroup for that afternoon's prom committee meeting.

"OK," Olivia announced. A huge, iridescent pendant of a butterfly bounced crazily on a copper chain around her neck as she spoke. "Everyone got it? We split up for one hour, sketch out ideas for the design, and then return here to discuss them. Good luck!"

Enid rose to her feet and headed over to a desk in the corner. She couldn't think of a single design element that fit the name Starlight Formal, which the group had already decided on using. She plopped down behind the desk and opened her sketch pad. The name seemed to go really well with the agreed-on old-fashioned theme. But what should the design be?

Staring at the blank sheet of paper, Enid held her pencil motionless in the air. She hadn't been able to come up with anything that didn't seem hopelessly overdone or too expensive to carry out. *A single white disco ball in the center of the ballroom?* she considered. *Maybe sheets of silver Mylar on the walls?* That seemed pretty cheesy— not elegant and old-fashioned at all.

Think old movies, Enid told herself. It shouldn't have been difficult. She loved old movies, and she watched the classic movie station on cable all the time. *Think Fred Astaire, Ginger Rogers, tuxedos, and top hats.*

Enid quickly made a sketch of an old cabaret she'd seen in a black-and-white movie. There was a many-tiered white box for the musicians to sit in, and a glittering silver railing surrounded the dance floor. Dozens of tables rose up on platforms around the center of the room with a balcony overhead. Enid knew it would be pretty, but she tore the sheet off her pad and crumpled it up. It would also cost thousands of dollars to create.

Someone cleared his throat, and Enid glanced up to see Blubber Johnson looking down at her. He seemed nervous, and he kept pulling awkwardly at the front of his T-shirt.

"Hi," Enid said, surprised to see Blubber. She hardly knew him.

"Hi, Enid," he replied shyly. "Uh . . . having

40

trouble?" he asked, pointing to the crumpled-up design in her hand.

Enid groaned. "*Big* trouble," she admitted. "I need to sketch a design for the prom decorations, but I can't think of anything."

Blubber pulled up a chair and sat down near Enid. He smiled nervously. "Well," he said, "I wouldn't know anything about decorating. I'm just here . . . I'm in the group that's gonna sell tickets."

He stared at Enid for a moment, looking absolutely terrified, but then he smiled quickly and licked his lips.

Why is he acting so strange? Enid wondered. *Is he . . . oh, gosh, could he actually be* flirting *with me? Weird!*

She knew very little about Blubber. He was on the football team—a linebacker, if she remembered correctly. And he wasn't exactly famous for his intelligence. Blubber had dark brown hair and brown eyes, and he was a *big* guy—he probably weighed something like 240 pounds. Most of his weight was solid muscle, but some of his mass hung over his belt. He had arms as thick as canned hams. He and Enid ran in such different social circles that it was odd he even knew she existed.

Blubber took a deep breath. "So . . . ," he asked tentatively, obviously searching for something to say, "so, what . . . what are you trying to do?"

Enid was pretty sure he wouldn't be able to help, but she wasn't coming up with any ideas on her own, and she always tried to be polite to everyone. "Well, the basic prom theme is Starlight Formal, and we want it to be elegant and old-fashioned. My job is to think up possible decorations to go with that theme." She gestured with her pencil at the blank pad. "But so far I haven't had much luck."

"El-Elegant," Blubber repeated, his face reddening slightly as he tripped over his words. "What's . . . what's that old-style design called . . . um . . . you know, from, like, before World War Two, like the Empire State Building?"

Old-style design? Enid wondered. *Does he mean . . .* "Art deco?" she asked out loud.

Blubber sighed with relief. "Yes!" he said. "That. That's elegant and old-fashioned, right? How about *that* as an idea?"

Enid was surprised to find herself feeling impressed at his suggestion. She'd studied the art deco movement in art history class—it was a design style focused on imitating the early industrial age, taking elements from factories, cars, and very urban cities with lots of curves, boxy structures, and gleaming steel. In fact, her favorite piece of architecture, the Chrysler Building, was an art deco design.

"You know," she said slowly, "that's not a bad idea at all."

Blubber smiled at her for a moment, but when Enid met his gaze, he quickly looked away. Enid felt a blush creeping up her neck. He *was* interested in her—she'd have to be blind not to see that. And she didn't know how she felt about his attention at all. She wasn't usually attracted to big guys, she had no interest in sports, and his lack of intelligence was definitely a major negative. But he *had* suggested the art deco idea, so he wasn't *totally* dim.

Now that Enid thought about it, art deco *was* a really good idea. It shouldn't be too difficult—or expensive—to create art deco arches out of silver Mylar on the walls of the ballroom, maybe with cutout silver stars. That even fit with the name of the prom! She felt herself getting excited as she got caught up in planning the design.

"You *really* think it's a good suggestion?" Blubber asked softly.

Enid immediately clamped down on any outward sign of her excitement—which he might take as her being overly friendly toward him. She certainly didn't want to give Blubber the wrong idea! "I think . . . ," she began, "I think it has possibilities."

Blubber would just have to be satisfied with that.

"Yuck!" Jessica blurted as she kicked her feet in her family's pool that afternoon. She held out a copy of a fashion magazine for Lila to see. The two girls were grabbing some late afternoon rays and flipping through magazines, scoping out possible prom dresses. "Check who's on the cover of *Flair* this month."

Lila peered over her sunglasses at the cover. "Ah," she said. "Would that be the horrible fashion witch, *Simone?*"

"*Yes,*" Jessica replied with a pout. She'd had a truly awful experience with that particular super-model when she'd been an intern at *Flair* maga-zine. The rivalry between Jessica and Simone had gotten way out of hand. "I can't believe they're still giving her covers," Jessica complained. "She's *evil.*"

"But beautiful," Lila replied, handing back the magazine to Jessica. "If you find *icicles* attractive. And obviously lots of guys do."

Jessica grimaced. "At least I have better memo-ries of that internship than just Simone," she said. "I wonder what's happening with Cameron in New York." Jessica had engaged in a brief romance with a guy named Cameron McGee during her tenure at *Flair,* but he'd moved to the New York branch of the magazine soon after they'd started dating. Falling in love with Cameron hadn't been easy—she'd been distracted trying to seduce Quentin Berg, a famous photographer, to forward her own modeling career before she'd finally ditched him for Cameron. "I can't believe I wasted so much time with Quentin," she continued. "Seeing two guys at once—what a mess."

"Hmmm," Lila murmured softly.

Lila's quiet sound seemed unusually subdued for her, so Jessica glanced at her friend. She was surprised to see a look of concern flickering on Lila's face.

"*What*, Li?" Jessica asked. "What's the matter? You're not jealous that I was dating two guys, are you? You know it's more trouble than it's worth—"

"No, no," Lila replied quickly. "Hardly." She stared down at the glimmering pool for a moment and then turned to Jessica, her brown eyes a little worried. "Jessica," she whispered, "have you thought of *one* possible prom date? The dance is coming up soon, you know."

Jessica groaned loudly and abruptly slid into the pool. As she let the water close over her head she thought, *Not Lila too! Why is everyone so concerned over me finding a date?* She popped her head out of the water and flicked back her wet hair. "Lila, relax," she instructed. "Finding a date is *not* going to be a problem for us! We've always been able to get any guy we wanted."

Well, almost, Jessica admitted to herself. She'd just have to put Devon Whitelaw in the category of "the one that got away"—even though that admission made her grind her teeth in frustration.

"I'm not concerned about finding a date," Lila protested. "I'm worried about finding the *right* date. You know how picky I am—it takes me weeks just to decide what earrings to wear for special occasions. And a date is a *much* more important prom accessory."

45

Jessica grinned and slapped the surface of the pool, splashing Lila.

"Quit it, Wakefield," Lila growled, kicking water back at her. "I'm serious."

"So?" Jessica asked. "What do you want to do about it? Nobody worthwhile has asked either of us yet. Should we start our prom date search now? I don't even know where to begin." She began treading water, concentrating the effort in her legs to exercise them.

Lila smiled. "I've come up with a plan to save us some time."

Jessica stopped paddling for a moment, thrilled with the smug look on Lila's face. Her devious best friend had obviously cooked up something cool! "What, Li?" she demanded. "Spit it out!" Jessica started to sink, so she began treading water again.

"Well, there are only a certain number of eligible guys at Sweet Valley High, no?" Lila peered at her fingernails, then flipped her hand over to view them from the palm side. "I figure it'd be helpful if we had a way of comparing them all to each other. So why don't we make a *list*?"

Jessica frowned. "A list?" she asked. "But we know all their names already—it's not like we didn't grow up with most of them."

"Ah, but this will be a special list," Lila continued. "Next to each name we'll write down all their particular features as honestly as we can, paying attention to their attributes, personalities, rumors—strengths and weaknesses. Then—"

"Then we'll put them in order," Jessica crowed with a grin. She flopped on her back and floated in the pool. "We'll *rank* them!"

"Exactly," Lila finished.

"It's brilliant," Jessica said. "It's absolutely perfect. This way whoever gets the number one spot on the list has the privilege of taking me to the prom!"

"Or *me*," Lila added.

Jessica sank to her feet so that just her head was sticking out of the water. She stood absolutely still, her eyes blazing at Lila. "Why should *you* get number one? It should obviously be me."

"Jessica," Lila said calmly, arching her eyebrows, "at this exact moment you look like a wet cat. And you're not being much smarter than one. Of course, *I* would get the guy on top of the list. No question about it."

Jessica laughed, stepping through the water toward Lila. She felt the endless rivalry between her and her best friend heating up, and she could never resist a challenge. "*You?*" she mocked. "You'll be lucky if you can get anyone in the top ten!"

"*Top ten?*" Lila squawked. "Are you *insane?* It is my right, as the most sophisticated girl in Sweet Valley, to have nothing less than number one! You bedraggled thing, you can't even afford a prom dress by a name designer!"

47

Jessica floated her palms on the surface of the pool, little ripples circling out from her quivering fingertips. "At least I *wear* my clothes—and I'm not worn *by* them!"

Lila gasped, taking a deep breath and arching her back in preparation to get really nasty. But before she could shoot another comment, Jessica suddenly saw a compromise.

"Wait, wait!" Jessica called, her adrenaline ebbing away. "We can list the guys together, but we'll *rank* them separately. We do have different tastes, after all, so our final lists will be different."

Swallowing whatever she was about to say, Lila relaxed her shoulders and nodded slowly. "OK," she conceded. "I *do* have higher standards than you. That should work. But what if there ends up being a tie?"

Jessica smiled. "Then we'll flip a coin," she replied with a shrug.

"Good," Lila agreed. "We'll *both* get our own personal number ones."

Hoisting herself out of the pool, Jessica slapped down on the tile beside Lila. "The list is an *excellent* plan," she said enthusiastically. "I'm glad I thought of it."

Lila glanced at her and snorted delicately. "*You* thought of it?" she asked archly.

Jessica stood up and began briskly toweling her hair. "What does it matter who thought of what?" she replied. "We've got work to do!"

Why are all my friends such slobs? Elizabeth wondered as she picked up soda cans and crumpled candy wrappers in the home ec room after the committee meeting had ended. *I'm the only one who even offered to clean up!*

She heard footsteps behind her. Elizabeth glanced up to see Enid entering the classroom. "Need any help?" Enid asked.

Elizabeth smiled at her best friend. "Sure," she replied. "I'm almost done anyway. I thought everyone else had abandoned me here to clean up by myself. And hey . . . I need to ask you for a ride home."

"Of course you can have a ride," Enid answered, her voice dropping to a whisper. "You know I'd never leave you here alone. I just . . . um . . . had to run to my locker to get something."

Elizabeth put down the soda cans she'd collected, immediately worried by Enid's tone. "What's the matter?" she asked.

Enid reddened and stooped to pick up a broken pencil. "I'm fine," she said quickly. "It's just . . . oh, it's nothing."

"Enid, look at me," Elizabeth ordered. Enid slowly stood up straight and met Elizabeth's gaze. "You listen to *my* problems all the time," Elizabeth continued gently. "Now it's my turn. *Tell* me."

For a moment Enid didn't reply—she lowered her head and began twirling the broken pencil in her fingers. Then she peered up at Elizabeth. "It's Blubber . . . uh, *Tad* Johnson. I just don't know what to think," she blurted in a rush. "Did you see him talking to me during the meeting? He was obviously interested in me. I mean, I *think* he was obviously interested in me. It's been a long time, but I'm sure I can still recognize flirting when I see it. But I'm pretty sure I don't want him to ask me to the prom . . . and I think he's going to!"

Elizabeth held up her hands in self-defense. "Whoa!" she cried. "Too much information at once."

"Sorry," Enid apologized sheepishly. "It's just been building up for the last hour or so."

"No problem," Elizabeth replied. "So let me see if I've got this straight. You're afraid Tad's going to ask you to the prom, and you don't want to go with him. Am I on track so far?"

"You got it," Enid said. "That's the problem in a nutshell."

Elizabeth sat on a nearby desk. "That is hard," she said thoughtfully. She sighed. "But if Tad asks you, at least you'll *have* a date. Unlike me."

"But I really don't want to go with . . . Tad," Enid told Elizabeth, obviously unused to using his real first name. She sat down on a chair and slumped into it. "And I don't want to hurt his feelings either."

Hurt feelings, Elizabeth thought, starting to feel sad thinking about her own prom situation. *I know*

50

all about those. "You'll figure out some way to let Tad down gently," she assured Enid. "But what am *I* supposed to do? Everyone's been giving me pressure to choose between Todd and Devon—but why should I think either of them even *wants* to be my prom date? Todd seems totally comfortable being friends, and Devon seems totally comfortable being strangers."

"That's an oversimplification," Enid argued. "You know Todd will always be crazy about you, and Devon . . ."

As Enid continued to give words of sympathy Elizabeth drifted off, thinking about Devon. How clearly she could remember the passion of his kisses, the warm taste of his breath, the salty sweetness of his lips . . . the intense gaze of his slate blue eyes, the way he seemed to be able to stare right into her very soul . . . the way his probing, thoughtful questions challenged her mind. . . .

Where is he right now? Elizabeth wondered. *Why does Devon feel so comfortable with the distance between us? Has he found someone else?* Her heart squeezed achingly.

"Earth to Elizabeth," Enid called. "Come in, Elizabeth!"

Elizabeth blinked and heaved a big sigh. "You know," she said glumly, "we both seem to be really unlucky in love lately." She turned to Enid and managed a weak smile. "But at least we have good friends."

Enid returned her smile. "If I dressed up in a tux, *I* could take you to the prom," she offered jokingly.

Elizabeth giggled, imagining her pretty, petite best friend in formal menswear. "You're not really my type," she shot back.

They laughed together for a moment. But Elizabeth couldn't maintain her happiness for more than a few seconds. She quickly stopped laughing and looked blankly at her friend.

Elizabeth almost gasped as she saw the painful loneliness in Enid's eyes—the dark emotions hit too close to home.

Enid quickly averted her gaze and stared down at her feet.

Elizabeth did the same. They sat in the classroom for a long, quiet moment, both of them lost in deep, private sadness.

Chapter 5

Devon stared miserably out his living room window at the bright sunlight shining down on the lush green grass of the front lawn. The beautiful Saturday afternoon did nothing to lighten his dismal mood. If anything, the cheerful view out the window made him feel *more* bored, lonely, and sad.

With a groan Devon pulled his legs up onto the padded window seat on which he was sitting. He rested his chin on his knees. *Moping around is so useless,* he reprimanded himself. Sure, he was occasionally prone to brooding, but being in a long-lasting funk like this made him feel like he was wasting his life. Still, no matter how he tried, Devon just couldn't shake the dark emotions churning inside him.

A delicious chocolate smell wafted into the living room, and Devon unfolded himself from the window seat with a sigh. He inhaled deeply, savoring the rich scent. *Nan must be making brownies,* he realized. *Maybe they'll help cheer me up.*

Wandering into the kitchen, he found Nan peering into the oven. She was wearing baggy blue slacks and a loose, floral-patterned pink blouse—covered by an apron as usual. Nan's hair had mostly gone gray, which wasn't surprising given her age, but she was still in good shape. She glanced up as he entered and favored him with a warm smile. "Hey, gloomy," she greeted him.

Devon didn't reply and instead perched on one of the tall stools that surrounded the island counter in the middle of the kitchen. He stared at the wooden countertop, tracing its ingrained patterns with a fingertip.

Nan closed the oven door with a slam. She placed a fragrant brownie pan on a metal rack to Devon's right.

Devon sighed again and reached for a nearby knife, planning to cut out a brownie for himself.

"Not yet," Nan warned. "They're not ready. They have to cool first, or you'll burn your tongue."

Devon let out a long groan. He tossed the knife down on the counter. "Of course," he muttered. "Of course I can't touch them. Just like everything else in my life—I can look, but I can't *have* any."

Nan blinked at him. "Anything you want to talk about?" she asked.

Devon shook his head and slumped his shoulders.

"Elizabeth," he whispered. After simply muttering her name, he had to press his lips together tightly and squeeze his eyes shut in order to swallow the devastating waves of emotion that suddenly threatened to overwhelm him. He ached all over with the effort.

Elizabeth, he thought, *you've totally screwed up my world. How could you do this to me? Can't you see we're meant to be together?*

He heard rushing water from the sink, and he opened his eyes to look. Nan had turned around and was washing a mixing bowl, wisely giving him time to sort himself out.

"It's not *fair*," Devon blurted. "Do you know how *pathetic* it is to know she's out there and that I can't talk to her? It's just . . . I think she's going to go with Wilkins to the prom. Not that I care about the prom, of course."

"Of course," Nan replied, raising her voice to be heard over the faucet. "But—"

"But *what?*" Devon challenged. "Can you tell me I'm wrong? That Elizabeth is eventually going to realize she loves me? That everything is going to work out? Because you know that's not true!"

"No," Nan replied, without turning to face him. She rinsed the mixing bowl. "That's not what I was going to say."

"Then what?" Devon asked sharply, sarcasm thick in his voice. "That it's better to have loved and lost than never to have loved at all? That's *lame*, Nan."

Nan froze for a moment. But then she relaxed and started washing again. "Huh," she said in a no-nonsense tone. "You keep on whining if it makes you feel better."

Devon bristled with irritation. "I am *not* whining," he contradicted her.

Nan just chuckled.

"Fine," Devon said, covering his eyes with his hands, pressing his fingers into his forehead. "*Fine.* So I'm whining. Sue me." He dropped his arms down onto the countertop. "But it still isn't fair."

Nan abruptly shut off the water. Then she turned around and shook a sudsy wooden spoon at Devon. His eyes opened wide as he saw the fierce expression on her face.

"Listen," Nan told him sharply. "Since when did you ever give two hoots about *fair?*"

"Since Elizabeth," Devon replied, crossing his arms over his chest.

Nan snorted in amusement. "Elizabeth is a lovely girl," she said, still holding out the wooden spoon as though she was going to smack him with it. "But I'm sick and tired of your bellyaching. Moping around the house like the world's coming to an end. Lying on the couch, moaning and groaning. You've become a big gob of self-pity. Well, I say enough. *Enough.*" Nan shook the spoon threateningly. "*Do* something."

Devon narrowed his eyes. Nan was right, and that made him feel belligerent. "Oh, good advice," he told her sarcastically. "Elizabeth won't talk to me—she barely *looks* at me. So just *what* do you expect me to do?"

Nan shrugged. "I'm sure I have no idea," she said. "But since when is Devon Whitelaw afraid to *fight* for what he wants?"

With that question Nan calmly turned around. She put the mixing bowl in a rack to dry and picked up another little bowl to scrub as though she'd never spoken at all.

I am not afraid to fight, Devon thought hotly, glaring at Nan's back. *It's just that Elizabeth holds all the cards, which really isn't fair. What am I supposed to do? I can't face her running away from me—*

Devon sat up straight on the stool. He was whining again. And it sounded childish even to himself.

When *had* he cared about the world being fair?

When *had* he ever been afraid to fight?

He'd lived through things that would have crushed a lesser man. He'd survived the death of his parents, his long search for a guardian. He'd even survived being pursued by Jessica Wakefield!

The beginnings of a smile played on his lips.

Elizabeth belongs with me, I'm sure of it, Devon told himself firmly. *And I'm not going to just stand around while Wilkins works his way back into her heart. It's time to take action.*

As Nan began to hum while splashing around in

the sink Devon's confidence seeped back, returning stronger than ever. And he started to plan. . . .

I have to be subtle, of course, he decided. *I can't make Elizabeth feel pressured at all. And if I have to play by her rules to win her back, then so be it.* He smiled grimly, inhaling a deep, fortifying breath.

But I will *win her back.*

Devon hopped off his stool. Then he walked over to Nan and gave her a quick kiss on the cheek.

"Oh," Nan said in surprise, pressing one soapy hand to the spot where he'd kissed her. "What was that for?"

"For being the wisest person I know," Devon replied. "Now I'm going to eat a brownie," he told her. "And I don't care if it burns my tongue. Any objections?"

"None at all." Nan smiled at him and winked. "Go for it," she said.

On Monday morning Jessica spotted Lila climbing out of her lime green Triumph convertible across the Sweet Valley High parking lot. Jessica quickly waved good-bye to Elizabeth and hurried to catch up to her best friend.

"Lila, *wait!*" Jessica called before Lila had managed to enter the school. Lila stopped and turned around, standing with her hands on her hips.

Jessica walked the last few feet over to Lila.

"Did you bring it?" she asked breathlessly.

Lila dug into her leather Prada backpack and pulled out her expensive camera. "Here," she said. "Now why was it so insanely important that I bring this to school?"

Jessica snatched the camera out of Lila's hands. After carefully checking to make sure there was film in it, she smiled, finally acknowledging that Lila had asked a question. "I have a plan," Jessica told her, feeling pleased with herself. "A *great* plan."

Lila groaned. "This isn't a get-rich-quick scheme, is it, Wakefield?" she asked suspiciously. "Because I'm *already* rich. And I don't need the aggravation that always seems to come with your 'great plans.'"

"You'll love this one," Jessica promised as they entered the school. "And it has *nothing* to do with money." She lowered her voice to a conspiratorial whisper. "You know that list we've been working on? Well, I thought of a way to make it even better."

Lila grabbed Jessica's arm and pulled her over to the relative privacy of a water fountain alcove. "How?" she demanded. "It's already good as it is."

Jessica grinned. "A brainstormed list of guys isn't enough," she told Lila confidently. "We need *visual* representation too. That way we can make a really informed decision about the guys. We'll be able to *see* them."

Lila pointed to the camera. "We'll take their *pictures,*" she murmured. "And add them to the list. Jessica, that's brilliant!"

"Thanks. Up-to-date pictures along with our descriptions," Jessica confirmed. "I thought it was pretty brilliant too. And there's no better time to start than the present. . . ."

Jessica bounded out of the water fountain alcove and immediately spotted Jeffrey French walking down the hall toward her.

"Wait!" Lila called. She hurried to catch up to Jessica. "Jessica," she said firmly, "give me the camera."

"Why?"

Lila held out her hand, wiggling her manicured fingernails impatiently. "*Because,* Wakefield," she replied, "you've never been able to take a picture in your life without cutting off someone's head or sticking your big thumb in the shot."

Jessica handed over the camera. Lila was absolutely correct—and besides, Lila was actually a decent photographer in her own right. Jessica had made Lila take modeling shots of her often enough, and they'd all come out very professionally. And it *was* Lila's camera, after all. "Good plan," she told her friend.

"Thanks," Lila drawled. "Now go corner Jeffrey before he escapes."

As Jessica stepped in Jeffrey's path to intercept him she was struck by how cute he was. Tall and blond, with dark green eyes, Jeffrey had the kind of lean, sexy body that came from playing soccer constantly. Too bad that inside he was as much a brainy, dull do-gooder as Elizabeth. In fact, Jeffrey and Elizabeth were incredibly similar in a lot of ways—they even *looked* vaguely alike. *Which is probably why they didn't last,* Jessica thought, thinking of the several months Elizabeth had dated Jeffrey.

"Yoo-hoo, Jeffrey!" Jessica called out as she approached him. "Smile at Lila!"

Jeffrey looked puzzled for a moment, but when he glanced at Lila and she raised her camera and pointed it at him, he posed and smiled. Lila took the shot.

"What was that for?" Jeffrey asked.

"Oh," Jessica replied lightly, "just memories. Junior year isn't going to last forever, you know, and I want to remember everyone who made it so special."

"Well, glad I could help," Jeffrey said with a smile. He turned away and headed down the hall.

"*That* was easy," Jessica told Lila when Jeffrey was out of earshot. "I hope they'll all go as smoothly."

"Don't count on it," Lila warned. "Who's next?"

"Um," Jessica murmured, searching the hall for their next subject. "There's Charlie Markus," she said, pointing toward a guy standing by his locker. Charlie had curly blond hair, hazel eyes, and a cute, freckled, upturned nose. "Hey, Charlie!" she bellowed down the hall.

Charlie looked over to her, surprised. He gently closed his locker as she and Lila hurried over to him. "Hey, Jessica. Hi, Lila," he greeted them pleasantly. "What's up?"

"Pose," Lila demanded. She raised the camera to her eye.

"Hey, wait!" Charlie protested. "What's this for?"

"Just quiet down and smile," Lila insisted.

In response Charlie held his hands up in front of his face.

Jessica groaned. Lila had made a big mistake— Charlie was a very nice guy, but Jessica knew he didn't take well to demands. Sometimes Lila didn't have the best *people* skills in the world.

"We just want to take your picture," Jessica told him soothingly. "No big deal."

Charlie backed up a step. "Oh, yeah?" he asked, his eyes narrowing suspiciously. "Do I get paid a modeling fee?"

Jessica felt completely annoyed with Lila for getting Charlie's guard up, but she forced herself to smile at him with all the charm she could muster—which was a considerable amount. She put her hand on his arm. "No," she breathed. "It's nothing like that, Charlie. We need your picture for . . . for a contest," she improvised. She peered up at him, batting her eyelashes. "And I promise— you'll *adore* the prize if you win."

Charlie rubbed the side of his face, thinking it over. "Well, I guess it's all right," he decided. "But Jessica, I know your schemes. If this picture shows up in a calendar or something, I'm *not* going to be happy."

"No schemes," she promised. "Not this time."

"OK," he said, turning to face Lila. "Let's do it."

As Lila set up the shot Jessica stepped back, feeling perfectly pleased with the way their plan had been progressing so far. *Two down,* she thought, *and . . . a bunch more to go. But I'm sure we'll get all the guys by the end of the day. They just can't resist the Wakefield charm!*

Charlie smiled, and Lila clicked the shutter. "Got it," she announced.

"That's it?" Charlie asked.

"See?" Jessica said with a grin. "That wasn't so bad, was it?"

"Not at all," Charlie replied. "Well, see ya." He walked off down the hall.

After he turned a corner, Jessica grabbed Lila's arms and shook her in excitement. "This is so much fun!" she cried.

"Wakefield, relax," Lila ordered. "You're agitating me." But Jessica could tell she was pleased with the way their plan was going too.

Jessica let Lila go and smiled. "You know," she said, "when we get it all together, we won't just have a list to choose from anymore. We'll have a catalog!"

And Jessica simply *loved* shopping by catalog!

Chapter 6

Elizabeth halted outside the door of Mata Hari's, an exclusive clothing boutique in downtown Sweet Valley, refusing to follow her twin inside. She crossed her arms over her chest and stood in place on the sidewalk.

I don't want *to shop for prom dresses,* Elizabeth thought stubbornly. *It's just a waste of time. All it will do is remind me . . . about things I'd rather not think about.* Besides, shopping really wasn't her thing—it was much more Jessica's department.

A second later Jessica pushed her way back out of the store, having finally realized that Elizabeth wasn't behind her. "Liz," she asked, sounding confused, "what are you doing just *standing* out here?"

Elizabeth let her arms dangle limply at her sides. Suddenly she felt tired and achy—the way she often felt when Jessica had managed to drag her on a shopping expedition. "I don't want to be here," she complained in an exhausted voice. "I just want to go home."

"Don't give me that," Jessica replied quickly. "C'mon, it'll be fun. Besides, I need your help."

"What do you need *me* for?" Elizabeth protested, but she allowed Jessica to grab her hand and lead her into Mata Hari's. "You've been shopping alone since you were two years old!"

Jessica giggled as the door shut behind them. "And that's not an exaggeration!" she agreed. "Well, nearly."

Elizabeth sighed. "How'd I let you talk me into this?" she moaned.

Jessica took both of Elizabeth's hands and met her gaze, her eyes twinkling with excitement. "Because you're a wonderful twin who knows when her sister needs help choosing a dress," she answered sincerely. "I've got a dozen picked out in here, and I can't decide. I need your opinion, Lizzie."

Elizabeth shook her head. "Where's Lila?" she asked. "And since when do you need *my* advice on clothes?"

"Lila had an appointment with her masseuse," Jessica replied. "And I've always valued your opinion on clothing, Liz. You have such a tasteful style. Understated but elegant."

"Lies," Elizabeth shot back. "You think my style is boring—you've always said so. You just didn't want to go shopping alone."

"OK!" Jessica chirped. She didn't even bother looking offended. "Whatever! Besides," she continued, smiling as she turned toward the racks of dresses, "you were obviously going to put off shopping until the last minute, and my twin *has* to look good at the prom. It's a reflection on me."

So that's it, Elizabeth thought. *Jessica doesn't want my opinion on her choices—she wants to make sure she has a say in what I'm going to wear! Well, she can just forget it. Neither Todd nor Devon is going to ask me anyway, so I'm boycotting the whole thing!*

Jessica pulled a long golden organza gown out of the rack. "What about this one?" she asked. "It's perfect for you. It would bring out the highlights in your hair."

Yuck, Elizabeth thought, eyeing the flouncy ruffled skirt of the gown with distaste. "I'd look like an exploding carrot in that," she told her twin.

"Just try it on," Jessica wheedled.

Elizabeth immediately plopped down on a nearby padded chair. "No way. I wouldn't wear that dress if you *paid* me."

After Jessica had hung the gown back on the rack, she turned to her twin with a hurt expression on her face. She bit her lip. "Why are you being such a spoilsport?" she asked. "This should be a big bonding moment between us, trying on dresses together for our junior prom. Why do you have to ruin it?"

Elizabeth sighed. "I just can't get excited about the prom, Jess," she admitted, feeling guilty about disappointing her twin. At least she owed Jessica an explanation for her attitude. "Todd and Devon have my mind spinning in circles. Every time I seriously consider going to the prom with one of them, I think about the other one, and I get all confused." She shook her head as Jessica returned to hunting through the racks. "And it's stupid to even think about *deciding* between them since basically I've been waiting around for one of them to ask me, and neither of them seems about to do that. So it's hopeless. And I just can't see the point of trying on prom dresses when—"

Jessica held up a shimmering pale lavender dress. "What about this one?" she asked.

"I told you, Jess, I don't . . ." She let her voice trail away as she got a good look at the dress Jessica was showing her. "Oh," Elizabeth said softly, rising from the chair. "That's gorgeous."

Jessica giggled. She thrust the lavender dress into Elizabeth's hands. Then she grabbed a white gown out of the rack and quickly rushed off toward the dressing rooms.

Elizabeth held up the lavender dress against her body and turned toward a nearby mirror. It was simply breathtaking. The pale lavender shimmered delicately and felt deliciously creamy to her touch. She cocked her head as she admired its cut in the mirror. The dress was elegant but not flashy, reminding Elizabeth of something she'd seen recently in one of Jessica's fashion magazines.

As she fingered the beautiful fabric of the dress she thought, *Todd would love it, that's for sure. He always thinks I look great in this color.*

Elizabeth didn't know how she felt about that particular observation, so she hung the dress on a hook beside the mirror and turned back to the rack to see what else she could find.

Her gaze immediately fell on a shorter, really sexy black dress she just knew Devon would die for. She quickly pulled it out and arranged it against her chest. This dress had thin strands of silver piping down its sides and a square-cut halter top with wide straps. It had a touch of antique elegance to it, but at the same time it was fully modern—and devastatingly hot.

Devon's never seen me dressed up, she realized. *I'd love to see the expression on his face when he sees me in this!* She could just picture the admiring look in his eyes. . . .

Then Elizabeth read the price tag . . . and gasped in shock!

Oh, wow, she thought, horrified. *I didn't even know it was* legal *to charge that much for a dress!*

She quickly hung the black dress on another hook by the mirror and reached for the lavender dress's price tag. Elizabeth shook her head ruefully as she read it. It was even more expensive than the black one!

Still, she thought as she pulled the dress down off the hook and held it up in front of herself again, *I'll only have one junior prom. It only happens once in a lifetime.*

Elizabeth quickly decided to try on both dresses. *Maybe the store will let me put them both on hold until either Todd or Devon asks me to the prom.* She gathered both dresses into her arms and headed toward the dressing rooms. If *they ask me,* she amended.

Just as Elizabeth had reached the dressing rooms Jessica burst out from one of the small stalls with a big grin on her face. "Well?" she demanded, holding out her arms in a statuesque pose. "What do you think?"

Elizabeth stared at Jessica in awe. She was wearing a pure white slinky sheath with rhinestones around the neckline and a long slit up the side. The dress fit snugly around Jessica's curves while revealing a sexy amount of shoulder. It made Jessica look like a confident, fully grown *woman* instead of the sixteen-year-old she was. Elizabeth couldn't remember ever seeing her twin look more gorgeous. "Just stunning," Elizabeth breathed. "You look absolutely beautiful."

Jessica posed in the dressing room mirror, grinning at herself. "I do, don't I?" she replied. "It's *perfection.*"

❖　　❖　　❖

"Hey, check this out!" Winston called to Todd and Ken Matthews across the tuxedo rental shop. "I've found what *I'm* going to wear!"

Todd turned to look and saw that Winston was wearing a giant plaid bow tie, the edges of which nearly reached the sides of his skinny shoulders. Todd guffawed loudly—the tie looked absolutely ridiculous and almost suited Winston's personality. "Hey, great choice," he told the class clown.

"You look hilarious in that," Ken added.

"Thanks," Winston said modestly. "I'd wear it, but Maria would probably kill me."

"I think you're right," Todd replied. "You'd better not."

"Hey, look!" Ken called. He reached up and pulled a "big man's" tuxedo jacket off a display hook and slipped it on. When he had managed to shrug his shoulders in, Todd could barely see his friend—the jacket simply engulfed him. It reached past his knees.

Ken turned around slowly, his blue eyes twinkling with laughter, the enormous jacket flapping around him. "What do you think? Do you think Olivia would go for this?"

"All *three* of us could fit in that," Todd noted with a laugh.

Winston rushed over and pretended he was a stuffy clerk taking Ken's jacket seriously. "A simply impeccable choice, sir," he fawned over Ken. He pulled the jacket up higher on Ken's shoulders and rearranged the giant collar. "You see how the cut of the shoulders accentuates your football player build?" Ken pretended to consider Winston's comment seriously in the mirror, cocking his head, and Todd was unable to stop from cracking up. "And the extra width of lapel suggests the body instead of offering it blatantly for display," Winston continued, slipping into a silly French accent. "Blatancy, it is not sex-zy. No? Your girlfriend, she will not be able to *reezist* you!"

Ken rubbed his chin. "You're so right," he replied. "I'd be an idiot not to grab it."

Todd shook his head with a grin. His friends were so goofy, but he was having a lot more fun on this trip to rent tuxedos than he'd thought. He'd been a little worried that going to rent a tux would get him thinking about Elizabeth. . . . Todd winced at the thought of her name. *That's exactly what I was trying* not *to do,* he told himself ruefully.

To distract himself, Todd grabbed a pair of perfectly horrible dress shoes off a nearby shelf and showed them to his friends. The shoes were made of dark red patent leather with big, gleaming silver buckles. Just looking at them made Todd feel dizzy. "Hey, guys!" he called. "I found my dancing shoes!"

"Eew," Winston said as he saw them, wrinkling up his nose. "If you don't get those, Wilkins, I'm never going to forgive you."

"They *eez* you," Ken said, attempting a French

accent too. But his accent was so much worse than Winston's—so truly lame—that it sounded like a Brooklyn accent spoken by a surfer dude. Todd really cracked up this time, and Winston joined in. Ken looked embarrassed for a second, but then he started laughing too.

Unfortunately their laughter was cut off abruptly when the *real* store clerk appeared beside them. "Excuse me, boys," the clerk said with withering scorn. "This is *not* a comedy club. If you're not serious about buying or renting anything, I'll have to ask you to leave."

Todd hastily put the shoes back on the shelf, and Ken quickly shrugged out of the vast jacket.

"Sorry," Winston told the clerk contritely. "We're serious. You won't hear us laugh again. Ever."

As the clerk stomped back toward the counter Todd had to remind himself not to look at Winston, or he was sure he'd start laughing again. Now that they'd been reprimanded, he felt an itch to laugh for absolutely no reason whatsoever.

Todd took a deep breath to steady himself and began to search through the racks in earnest. *An old-fashioned tuxedo,* he thought as he looked for his size. *But not too old-fashioned. Think classic.*

"Todd," Ken whispered next to him. *"Help."*

Todd looked over at his friend and saw an expression of pure confusion on Ken's face. "What's the matter?" Todd asked.

Ken gestured to a display of various ties and cummerbunds in all different styles and colors. "The tuxedo's easy," Ken explained. "I'll just get a basic one in my size. But how in the world am I supposed to pick a tie? Or a cummerbund?"

With a smile Todd patted his friend on the shoulder. "It's easy," he answered. "My father explained it to me. You just match the tie and cummerbund to whatever color your date's dress is going to be. Or you can just get black or white, which go with everything."

Ken scratched his nose, thinking it over. "I guess I'll just get black," he decided. "Who *knows* what Olivia's going to come up with—probably something way funky and colorful. There's no way I'd be able to match her, and she won't tell me what she's going to wear anyway. It's supposed to be a surprise. So black it is." Ken looked very relieved at having made a decision.

"That sounds like the safest bet," Todd told him.

"Good," Ken said. "Black is fine with me. Olivia expects me to be plain and dependable like always, so I guess I can't go wrong with black." He paused for a moment. "I've got to rent shoes too. But I think I can handle *that* on my own."

"OK," Todd agreed. "I'll be over here. And hey—where's Winston?"

Both guys glanced around, but Winston had vanished.

Ken shrugged. "He's probably in the changing room. He wouldn't have gone far."

"I guess not," Todd replied.

As Ken headed over toward the racks of shoes Todd turned his attention to the tie-and-cummerbund display. His gaze immediately alighted on a tie of a light blue color.

Elizabeth will probably wear a pastel color, he thought.

Todd sighed as he reached up for the tie and found a matching cummerbund. He knew he was getting ahead of himself—planning his tuxedo on what Elizabeth would probably wear when he wasn't even sure if they were going to the prom together yet. *But maybe if I rent this blue stuff,* he reasoned, *then it'll actually force me to find the guts to ask her. I'll be one step closer anyway.*

Just then Winston burst out of the changing room. Todd stared at his friend in amazement. Winston had tried on a *really* old-fashioned tuxedo—with a ruffled shirt and tails and everything. He even had a short top hat perched on his head, and he was twirling a sleek black cane in one hand.

"Ta-da!" Winston announced. He tipped his hat to both Todd and Ken, bowing deeply.

"That looks *great,*" Todd said enthusiastically.

"Yeah," Ken agreed. "Funny but still *right.*"

Winston tossed the cane a short distance into the air and caught it again. "I know," he told them with a grin. "I'll take it!"

A little while later all three guys had picked out tuxedos and had left them with the clerk for alterations, which would be completed in a few days. As they left the store Todd felt happier than he'd been in weeks. Plans for the prom were in motion—plans for him and Elizabeth. If everything continued like this, he figured Elizabeth would get swept up easily in those plans along with him. And eventually she wouldn't be able to say no like he feared. Her going to the prom with him would be . . . inevitable.

Todd followed his friends down the street in downtown Sweet Valley, heading toward Todd's BMW. *It's going to be a perfect prom,* Todd thought. *And I'm going to have the best date there*—

He stopped short on the sidewalk when he caught sight of two blond girls inside a dress boutique he was passing. It was Jessica . . . and Elizabeth.

Todd's breath caught in his throat. Both of the twins were dressed up to the nines in amazing dresses, but Elizabeth . . .

Ken whistled, and Todd blushed. He had never seen Elizabeth looking more beautiful. She peered at herself in a mirror and held up her hair to see how it would look. Her dress was long and shiny, and it made her look so . . . soft, as though she was slightly out of focus. *Lovely,* Todd thought, his heart hammering in his chest. And just as he'd guessed, her dress was a shimmering pale lavender.

I knew it, Todd told himself. Reluctantly he turned away from the store window before Elizabeth or Jessica spotted him. As he started following Winston and Ken toward his car again, he sighed happily. *It's all coming together,* he thought. *And it's only a matter of time before Liz and I are at the prom together, dancing in each other's arms. Like we should be.*

Chapter 7

"Do you think Bruce Patman *still* kisses like a dead jellyfish?" Jessica asked Lila. Way back at the beginning of the school year Jessica had written an article for the *Oracle* about all the bad dates she'd had—and told the world just what she'd thought of Bruce's kissing style. She hadn't used his real name, but everyone still knew who she was writing about. But she hadn't kissed the rich, handsome, *exasperating* senior in a very, very long time.

"Well," Lila said as she pulled a piece of paper out of the sheaf of notes on her lap, "he's kissed a lot of girls since you dated him, Jess. How long ago was that? It feels like a *decade* ago or more. Perhaps he's improved since then."

Jessica sat up on the edge of the couch in the Wakefield den. "Probably not," she decided. "But, oh, I'll give him the benefit of the doubt." She bent over and scribbled something on her page of notes. "I put down that he kisses like a *live* jellyfish," she told Lila.

Both girls giggled.

"OK," Lila said firmly, breaking off their merriment. "*Peter DeHaven.* I already put down that he's handsome and serious, with dark brown hair and hazel eyes, and that's he's good at science. Now I need something to put in his key word category. Any ideas?"

"How about *cruel?*" Jessica suggested. "He was awful to Joanna Porter, even though he really liked her. Besides, cruel isn't necessarily a turnoff—it just depends on how much of a challenge you want."

"Cruel it is," Lila replied, scribbling on her Peter DeHaven page. "What did you write for Bruce's key word?"

"*Arrogant,* of course," Jessica answered with a big grin. "What else could it possibly be?"

Lila laughed. "What did you write for Aaron Dallas's best feature and worst feature?"

"Let's see. . . ." Jessica quickly thumbed through the pages of notes she was holding as she crossed her legs on the couch. "Here it is: 'Aaron Dallas. OK, best feature? Great legs. Gotta love those soccer boys' legs!' And worst feature? Um . . . I wrote down *cranky.*"

"He *does* get snippy sometimes," Lila agreed with a snort of amusement. "Listen to what I wrote about Bob Hillman. . . . 'Cute, with thick, wavy blond hair and green eyes. Thinks his smile can get him anything he wants—but it might look good in a prom photo. Plus points for being a member of Sweet Valley Country Club. Minus points for being a shallow creep.'"

"Good!" Jessica approved. "Key word?"

"That was trickier," Lila admitted. "So I simply put down *avoid*."

"Sensible choice," Jessica replied. "Now, for Paul Jeffries's key word I wrote *womanizer*. But I'm not sure that's fair. I mean, I've dated more than he has, and nobody calls me a *manizer*."

Lila smirked. "Are you sure, Jess?"

Jessica gasped. "What do you mean? What did you hear?"

"Oh, nothing . . ."

"Tell me!" Jessica insisted. She smacked Lila on the shoulder.

"Do not hit me, Jess," Lila seethed. Then she sighed. "No, nobody calls you a *manizer*, Jessica. It's a stupid word anyway."

"Good," Jessica said.

Lila grinned. "Of course, they *do* call you something else. . . ."

"What?"

Peering at her nails as though she'd suddenly lost interest, Lila cleared her throat. "I forget," she replied.

"Lila . . . ," Jessica warned.

"Oh, it doesn't matter," Lila continued blithely. "Just put down *womanizer* for Paul. It's close enough to the truth."

Jessica poked her friend on the arm with her finger. "C'mon, Li," she begged. "Tell me what everyone calls me."

Lila stared directly into Jessica's eyes. "They don't call you anything," she answered, shaking her head in fake sorrow. "I can't remember the last time I heard you spoken about. In fact, I'm sorry to tell you that most people don't even know you exist."

"That is such a lie!" Jessica replied huffily. "I'm incredibly popular, and I know it. Tell me what they really say."

"Please," Lila complained. "I'm sorry I said anything. It was supposed to be a joke. Can't you just drop this?" She shook her pad of paper. "Remember, we have the list . . . and we're almost done."

"OK, OK," Jessica conceded, frowning. "Who's left?"

Lila consulted her list. "Huh. I'm all done with my guys. Any categories left for any of your names?"

"Just one," Jessica replied, peering at a sheet of notepaper. "Tim Nelson. And all I need about him is his best feature."

"What's his *worst* feature?" Lila asked.

"Uh . . ." Jessica checked what she'd written.

Elizabeth was always after her to work on improving her handwriting, and as Jessica tried to decipher her own chicken scratch she admitted to herself that her twin might have a point. "Let's see. . . . Well, he's on the football team, right? But worse, he, like, *lives* the football team. It's all he thinks about. So his worst feature—he's a total mindless jock."

"OK, then," Lila said. "Best feature, total mindless jock. There are times when mindlessness comes in very handy. Sometimes you just want big and stupid."

"Cool," Jessica replied with a giggle as she wrote it down. "Tim Nelson—best feature and worst feature, total . . . mindless . . . jock." She waved the list in the air. "And . . . we're done! This was the most fun I've had all year! We should have thought of making a catalog ages ago!"

"We're not quite done," Lila reminded her. "We still have to put the list with the pictures and then rank them. But that's the fun part—we've finished getting all the facts together."

"Oh," Jessica said with a dismissive wave of her hand, "that'll be no problem. We've done excellent work today, and I think we deserve a break." She gathered the pages of Lila's list and added them to her own. "Celebratory shake at the Dairi Burger? I'm in the mood for greasy fried food and milk shakes. Who should we call and invite to our celebration?"

Lila was already reaching for her backpack. She

grabbed it and pulled out her cellular phone. "You call Amy; I'll call Sandy and Jeanie."

Less than a minute later Jessica had spoken to Amy and hung up the phone. "Amy was just heading out," she explained to Lila. "She was already on her way over there. Our friends are *so* predictable."

"Jeanie's mother said Jeanie and Sandy had already headed out too," Lila reported, flipping her phone shut. "Let's motor."

Jessica grabbed the pages of the list and pressed them to her chest. "I can't wait to see the looks on their faces when they see this," she breathed. "Everyone's going to be so jealous— we're geniuses!"

An expression of pure alarm crossed Lila's face. "Hold it there, *genius*," she said. "Hello! We can't show anybody this list! Do you know what would *happen* to us if it got out?"

Jessica's mouth dropped open as she considered the possibilities. Some of the guys might actually be hurt by the things she and Lila had written about them. Especially the worst feature category. "Oh, wow," she muttered. "I guess not everybody would think it's a good thing."

"Remember the slam books?" Lila asked. Earlier in the school year a bunch of girls had gotten together and written really personal observations about their friends in little notebooks. But when the identities of the writers leaked out, it had been a disaster of epic proportions. Huge fights and torn friendships had swept the halls of SVH. "Honesty has a way of going over like a lead balloon."

"Too true," Jessica replied. "What was I *thinking?*" She stood up and stuffed the list inside her chemistry notebook that was lying on an end table in the den. *It'll be safe enough in there,* she thought with a chuckle. *Anyone who* wants *to see the periodic table of the elements* deserves *a rude shock!*

"C'mon, Jessica," Lila commanded, opening the front door. "If we don't get there quick, our friends are going to start talking about us. And you know how catty some girls can be."

"Not at all like us," Jessica said, following her friend out the door.

"Not at all," Lila replied.

Elizabeth looked up from her laptop computer in her bedroom when she heard a car horn blaring outside. *What time is it?* she thought, hastily glancing at her watch. It was four-thirty. Winston and Maria were supposed to pick her up to go to the country club to check out their facilities for the prom—now. *Oh, no! I totally lost track of the time!*

She quickly saved the *Oracle* article she'd been engrossed in, stood up, and peered out the window. Sure enough, Maria's car was sitting in the driveway. Through the window she could just make out Winston sitting in the driver's seat, with the shadowy form of Maria sitting beside him.

Elizabeth groaned as she bent down to put on her shoes. She'd promised herself that she'd write up a checklist of what to look for in the country club's ballroom—things like space for the disc jockey, where to set up the buffet, and how many tables they could fit around the dance floor. But she'd gotten so involved with her *Oracle* article that she'd forgotten to make the checklist . . . and now she would have to wing it.

If there's anything I truly hate, Elizabeth thought as she laced up her shoe, *it's being unprepared.*

The car horn honked again, and Elizabeth quickly checked her hair in her bedroom mirror. It was weirdly fluffed up from playing with it as she was writing. Suddenly she realized she'd left her headband in the den earlier.

On her way downstairs she heard the car horn blare again. *Winston sure does love to honk that horn,* she thought, gritting her teeth. "Hold your horses," she muttered. "I'm coming!"

She hurried to search the den—but her headband wasn't to be found. *Jessica must've taken it,* she realized. *What a shocker. Oh, well. My friends can deal with seeing my hair a mess.* Elizabeth patted her hair down as best she could and rushed toward the front door.

But after taking only one step out the door, she stopped short. *You know,* she thought, *I should probably bring something to write on in case I need to take notes.* She turned around and sprinted back inside. *I'm so unprepared for this, it makes me sick!*

Elizabeth was planning to rush up to her room and grab one of her pads of yellow paper, but Winston honked the horn again. So instead she glanced frantically around the den. She spotted Jessica's chemistry notebook on an end table, sprinted over, and grabbed it.

Jessica won't mind, she thought. *Knowing how my twin takes notes, it's probably full of blank pages anyway!*

Then Elizabeth headed out the door, accompanied by the nonmusical sound of Winston's horn.

Chapter 8

Todd stared at Elizabeth's feet.

How does she keep her sneakers so clean? he wondered as he held steady the ladder that she was standing on. She was taking measurements of one of the ballroom's walls to see how large a banner they would need for the prom. *If I had canvas sneakers,* he mused, *they'd probably be grass-stained or covered with mud. Anyway, they certainly wouldn't be clean enough to . . . kiss.*

He let his gaze travel up past her sneakers. *She has such cute ankles,* he thought. The muscles under her tan skin stretched as she reached to hold up the measuring tape, and Todd's mouth went dry. It was such a lovely movement. He felt struck with a sudden desire to run his finger along the line of her anklebone. Maybe she wouldn't even notice.

Todd shook his head. *No, don't be stupid,* he told himself. She'd probably think his touch was a bug or something and kick him. Even if she knew that he had touched her ankle, she probably wouldn't be pleased. But he was getting so frustrated! Being so close to her and not being able to touch her was absolute torture.

I should never have asked her to marry me, Todd berated himself. *What was I thinking? We're only sixteen!* It had been way too much too soon. No wonder she'd gone running away from him, needing her space. But he'd been so desperately afraid of losing her to that jerk Devon Whitelaw that he'd temporarily lost his mind and had acted drastically.

And now I can't even touch her ankle, Todd thought miserably. *I really blew it this time.*

Elizabeth shifted on the ladder and the cuff of her pale jeans rode upward, revealing even more skin. He sighed. *Just one touch,* he argued with himself, unable to squelch his desire to run his finger along her ankle. *Just one.*

He removed one hand from the ladder—at the same time Elizabeth repositioned her feet. The ladder wobbled, and he had to grab it again, holding it steady.

"Having problems down there?" Elizabeth called.

Todd blushed furiously. "N-No," he stuttered, but then he decided to be daring. "I was just blinded for a second by your attractive ankles."

For a moment Elizabeth didn't respond, and Todd held his breath, worrying that he'd offended her.

But then she cleared her throat. "Todd," she scolded, "*please* pay attention to the measurements I'm calling down. I don't want to have to do this again."

Todd smiled. Anyone else might have been stung by Elizabeth's scolding, but he'd known her long enough to know when she sounded pleased, so he knew his compliment had hit home. He felt almost as warmed by her reprimand as if she'd told him she loved him.

"Hey," he called up, "what are you measuring for anyway? What's going on this wall?"

"I told you, a banner," she replied, grunting as she stepped up a rung on the ladder.

"What's it going to say?" Todd asked. He changed the position of his hands on the ladder to accommodate her shift in weight.

"I'm not sure," Elizabeth admitted. "Something like Welcome to the Starlight Formal, I guess. I'm going to leave the particulars to the artists in the design committee."

"How about the wall we measured first?" Todd persisted.

"The one behind me, across the ballroom?"

Todd nodded, but he realized she couldn't see him from her position up above. "Yes," he said.

"What was with all the crazy measuring you were doing over there?"

"Well, Enid came up with this amazing art deco design," Elizabeth answered, obviously warming to the subject. She stretched her arms wide as she spoke, holding the measuring tape against the wall. "We're planning to put up a giant silver Mylar crescent moon against a stark black background," she explained. "We're going to cut tiny stars out of the moon and put those up all along the backdrop. Enid's got a pattern all worked out."

"That sounds cool," Todd said, hoping Elizabeth would keep talking.

She did. "We're supposed to have a single white spotlight on the moon, which should make it sparkle. And then in the center of the ballroom we're going to hang a disco ball but only train white lights on it. That way we can get the old-fashioned mood without losing the lights that make dancing more fun."

Todd could easily picture himself and Elizabeth slow dancing together in the atmosphere she was describing. He closed his eyes as he thought about Elizabeth in her beautiful dress resting her head against his chest. The dance floor would clear out as the single spotlight moved off the moon and illuminated the two of them dancing alone in the darkness. Everything else in the room faded into the background as the image of the two of them gently twirling played in his mind. Nothing else mattered except how happy he would feel dancing with Elizabeth in his arms.

He sighed, opening his eyes. Todd had been having a good time working with Elizabeth all afternoon. They were getting along better than they had since Devon first moved to town.

Todd glanced up at her. She was frowning in concentration, peering at the tiny numbers on the measuring tape in her outstretched hands. Elizabeth looked beautiful. She didn't need to dress up to win his heart, even though she looked amazing when she did dress up. Even as simply dressed as she was now, in jeans and a T-shirt, she was the girl of his dreams. He loved what she'd done to her hair today too—even though he couldn't have said what was different. It looked tousled and fuller somehow. Lovely.

"Todd, write this down," Elizabeth instructed him from her perch on the ladder. "Seven feet long, two feet wide."

Holding the ladder steady with one hand, Todd pulled a small notepad out of his pocket. He braced the notebook on one of the rungs and scribbled down the numbers she'd told him.

But his mind wasn't on the measurements. He was feeling so close to Elizabeth, so connected. They were alone together for the first time in weeks, and she couldn't run away—she was trapped on the ladder. Even his comment about her ankles had gone over well! He knew it would be the perfect moment to ask her to the prom.

"You get that, Todd?" Elizabeth asked.

"Uh, yeah. Sure," he replied. He coughed gently, clearing his throat. *C'mon!* he instructed himself. *Just ask her!*

Why was he so nervous? Above him was the girl who he'd dated for nearly the whole school year, the girl who knew all his secrets, the girl who he trusted more than any other person on earth. So what was he afraid of?

He knew the answer to that, all right. He was afraid she might look pityingly down on him. Tell him that she'd made her choice—that she was in love with Devon Whitelaw. He was terrified that she might say no.

Todd took a deep breath, steeling himself. *Sometimes you just have to cut through the fear and take a risk,* he decided. *The bigger the goal, the bigger the risk. And this is a huge risk—your heart's on the line. But Elizabeth . . . Elizabeth is worth it.*

"Um," he began tentatively. "Uh, Liz?"

"Yes?" she asked, sounding distracted.

"Do you think . . . I mean, would you—"

The rest of his sentence was cut off by the sound of the ballroom's metal door being flung open with a big clang. Todd turned quickly to glare at whoever had ruined his big moment.

It was Devon.

Todd narrowed his eyes and seethed. *What's* he

doing here? Todd thought hotly. *Doesn't he have anything better to do than show up and ruin my life?*

"Sorry," Devon apologized to everyone in the ballroom, who had turned to stare at him. "I didn't think the door would swing open like that."

"No problem!" Winston shouted from the other end of the room. "C'mon in! We can use all the help we can get!"

Traitor, Todd silently accused Winston, which he knew was unfair. But he wasn't feeling completely rational at the moment. Devon had a way of making Todd feel furious and powerless at the same time. It was not a sensation Todd liked.

Devon waved at Winston but looked around the room before entering. He quickly spotted Elizabeth on the ladder.

Don't come over here, Todd thought. *Don't.*

In spite of Todd's hostile vibes Devon sauntered toward the ladder. "Hi," he called up to Elizabeth when he reached them. He ignored Todd completely, which only made Todd feel like bashing Devon in the head with his fists.

Calm yourself, Todd thought. *Remember, your fight with Devon was what made Elizabeth break up with both of you in the first place. So whatever you do,* don't *lose control!*

"Hi," Elizabeth replied to Devon quietly. "What brings you here?"

Devon shrugged. "I was just sitting at home,

95

bored—so I thought I'd come over and see if any-body needed any help. So . . . do you need any help?"

Todd had to press his lips together to keep from laughing out loud. It was so obvious what Devon was trying to do! He didn't want to help at all—he was just here to see Elizabeth, to fool her into liking him. And that was the *only* reason. No *way* would Elizabeth fall for such an obvious trick.

But Todd stared in shock as Elizabeth smiled at Devon. "That's so sweet," she told him, leaning toward him.

The ladder wobbled alarmingly, and Todd had to grab it to steady her.

Todd rested his head against the ladder after he had gotten it under control. A blind person could see how strong Elizabeth's feelings for Devon were—they were making her nearly fall off ladders.

I guess this isn't *the perfect moment to ask her to the prom,* Todd thought miserably. *And I'm starting to think that moment's never going to come. Not with Devon Whitelaw in the picture.*

"The country club supplies a choice of two differently shaped tables—round or rectangular," Enid informed Olivia, Maria, and Winston, who were standing beside her in a corner of the ballroom. "What type should we ask for? And how should we arrange them?"

Enid turned along with the others to stare out

96

into the ballroom, contemplating her questions. Circular tables, in a random pattern all around the ballroom, might look nice. But there was also something to be said for long tables arranged artfully. . . .

"I've got an idea," Winston said. He grinned goofily. "What if we get lots of long tables and put them in a circle—like a wagon train around a campfire? That would be a perfect homey touch."

Maria shook a fist at him. "Get serious, Egbert," she warned, "or you're going *stag* to the prom."

"I'll be good," Winston peeped, holding up his hands defensively.

Enid and Olivia laughed—but Enid immediately fell silent when she saw Blubber Johnson heading her way.

She groaned. Ever since she'd spoken with him at the committee meeting the other night, Blubber had been following her around like a lovesick puppy dog. He hadn't yet asked her to go with him to the prom, but she feared it was only a matter of time until he managed to gather enough bravery to do it.

And Enid had no idea how she was going to let him down gently.

"Um, Enid?" Blubber asked nervously when he had reached the group. "You know how you asked me to get all those supplies? Well, I need to write them down, or I'm going to forget something. But I—I don't have any paper. Do you?"

"Sure!" Enid chirped. She hadn't brought a

notebook with her, but she was going to take any excuse she could find to get away from Blubber. "Winston brought a notebook, but he left it . . . over there." She gestured vaguely toward the other end of the ballroom. "Didn't you, Win?"

Winston's face screwed up in confusion. "I don't remember bringing—"

"Of course you did," Enid interrupted. She nodded deliberately so he'd get the hint. "Now let's go get it." She opened her eyes wide, pleading silently for him to understand.

Winston shrugged. "Sure, whatever," he replied.

Enid grabbed Winston's arm and began leading him across the room. To her chagrin Blubber followed along.

"No," she told Blubber, gently but firmly. "You stay here and find out if Maria or Olivia needs anything else added to the supply list. We'll be back in a second with some paper for you."

Blubber obediently turned around.

"What was that all about?" Winston whispered when they were out of earshot.

Enid sighed. "I'm being horrible," she answered, "but he's driving me crazy. He's working up to asking me to the prom, and I don't think I'll be able to handle that gracefully."

"Oho," Winston replied with a nod. "You're not into Blubber, huh? Why not? He's a decent enough guy."

Enid shook her head ruefully. "I know," she

said. "That just makes it worse. He's just not my idea of a dream prom date. I feel *terrible* about it, but lying to myself—or him—would just make things worse."

"I guess that makes sense," Winston said diplomatically. "So now where do we find paper? I *didn't* bring a notebook, you know."

"I have no idea," Enid admitted. "Look around. Somebody had to have brought *something* we can use."

Winston pointed to a notebook leaning against the wall by the ballroom door. "Over there," he said.

They hurried over to the notebook, and Enid picked it up. "Jessica Wakefield," she read off the cover. "Chemistry. Oh, Elizabeth must've brought this. I'm sure she won't mind if we rip out a few sheets." Enid flipped open the cover, and a small stack of papers that were clipped together fell out onto the floor.

Winston bent to pick up the stack. As he started reading the top sheet his eyes grew wide.

Enid glanced over his shoulder at the papers he was holding. She gasped as she read, and she felt a little sick to her stomach. In what was obviously Jessica and Lila's handwriting was a list of all the single guys in Sweet Valley High—with descriptions of each of them. Really *personal* descriptions!

Winston chuckled as he flipped through the pages. "It goes on and on," he said. "No single guy is spared. Too bad I have Maria. I'd love to read up on me."

The nerve of those two! Enid thought hotly. She'd never had any particular love for Jessica or Lila, but . . . "I can't believe they did this," she told Winston.

He grinned at her. "Oh, no?" he replied. "*I'm* not surprised at all."

Enid laughed. "I guess you're right," she admitted. "Those two are capable of anything."

"I'll take care of this," Winston said, a mischievous smile on his face. He slid the list under his shirt.

"Win," Enid protested nervously, "don't you think you should put that back—"

She fell silent as she noticed Blubber breaking away from Maria and Olivia and heading in her direction. Enid couldn't bear facing him again—his nervous stuttering, his worried eyes, his eagerness to please all made her want to run for it.

"Oh, gosh," she said. She grabbed Winston's arm. "Just tell him I had to go, OK? Tell him I wasn't feeling well. Tell him anything!"

"What?" Winston cried, sounding bewildered. "Who?"

But Enid was already fleeing out the door.

"Ooh!" Elizabeth sang, her head thrown back.

Devon grinned at her. "That's beautiful, Elizabeth," he teased her gently. He knew she was just testing the acoustics of the ballroom, trying to find the best place to situate the disc jockey, but she sounded so silly, he couldn't help giving her grief about it.

"Shut your trap," Elizabeth told him, stifling a giggle. "I *have* to do this. Or would *you* like to take over?"

"No, no," he protested with a smile. "You're doing a great job, I swear."

She elbowed him in the side and moved on to test another spot in the ballroom.

As Devon followed her he thought about how good it felt to be with her again, even if they weren't alone, even doing something as unromantic as testing sound levels. The simple fact of her presence soothed him, once again making him feel glad to be alive.

He smiled to himself as he remembered the way she'd ditched Todd just a few minutes after Devon had arrived. *Well,* he amended, *what she said was, "Todd, I really need you to help Tad with the supply list."* But that was obviously a ditch, and that was absolutely fine with Devon. The *last* thing he wanted was Wilkins hanging around, staring balefully at him.

"Ooh!" Elizabeth began singing again, and Devon shook his head in fake dismay.

She laughed, breaking off her sound testing. "Stop it!" she told him, shaking a finger at him. "Don't make me laugh, I'm warning you!"

"Or what?" Devon challenged.

"Or . . . I'll put you in charge of finding the deejay."

"Good," Devon said, surprising himself. *I'll do anything to help her,* he realized. *Anything she needs.* "I'd be glad to do that. In fact, I volunteer."

"Really?" Elizabeth asked. "Do you mean it?"

"I said so, didn't I?" Devon replied. "Why do you sound so surprised?"

"Sorry," she said quickly. "I think it's great—one less thing for me to worry about. But I am a little surprised," she admitted. "I wasn't expecting you to want to get so involved. You've only been at SVH for a short time, and—"

Devon sighed. "To be completely honest, I have ulterior motives," he said, looking away from her face, worried about how she'd react to what he was going to say. "Usually I think things like school spirit are a total waste of time. But I can tell how important this prom thing is to everyone at Sweet Valley High—especially to you—and . . ." He took a deep breath and met Elizabeth's eyes. For a second she looked like a rabbit caught in a pair of headlights. It was a reaction he was used to—very few people could meet and hold his gaze. But then she relaxed with a tiny exhaled breath, really listening to him. "And I need to make friends," he continued. "I'm tired of being a loner."

He broke off their eye contact, staring out into the airy ballroom. "You probably think that's really cynical of me."

Elizabeth put her hand on his arm. He flinched

as her touch sent a tingling shock into his body, shivering down to his toes. "Not at all," she told him firmly. "In fact, I'm impressed."

That surprised Devon. "Impressed? But I'm just out to get what I want. Why should that impress you?"

"I've always thought that the best way to make friends is to pay attention to what people find important and then offer your time to help them out," she answered sincerely. "Sure, the end result might be for your own benefit, but what does that matter as long as you really do help?"

"In this case," Devon quipped, "the *means* justify the *end*."

Elizabeth laughed.

Devon inhaled deeply as a feeling of happiness warmed his chest. How he loved the sound of her laughter; how he loved that she could make him *think*. Elizabeth made him feel like a better person just by being near her. And how he longed to kiss her at that moment!

Elizabeth smiled at him and met his gaze briefly before turning away, her hands fluttering nervously. She headed toward her next spot to test the acoustics.

Devon followed, a grin plastered on his face. *Playing by her rules was obviously a good idea,* he congratulated himself. *My plan seems to be working perfectly.*

Chapter 9

"What do you mean, you can't find the catalog?" Lila screeched at Jessica in the school hallway on Wednesday morning. Lila slammed her locker shut with a bang. "If anyone gets their hands on that, we'll be socially ruined! Jessica Wakefield, you're the most irresponsible, scatterbrained—"

"Lila! You're making a scene!" Jessica hissed.

"So?" Lila demanded. "I'll make a scene if I want to make a scene!"

"It's not the good kind of scene," Jessica replied. "You don't want anyone asking what's wrong, do you? What will you say then?"

Lila crossed her arms over her chest. "I'll just explain that my so-called best friend is *mentally deficient* for losing the catalog we'd—" Lila paused. "Oh," she finished in a normal tone of voice. "I see your point. Don't want to go there."

"Right," Jessica told her. "And anyway, Li, as I was about to say before you freaked out, the only person who could possibly have my notebook is Liz. And while she might be horrified if she reads it, she's certainly not going to *show* it to anyone."

"How can you be so sure?"

"It's just not like her," Jessica argued. "She's the *good* twin, remember? She'll never snitch on me except in matters of life and death. Believe me, it's something I've counted on my whole life. Sure, I might have to listen to a lecture from her, but I'm positive the list is safe."

Lila sniffed, but Jessica could tell she was partially mollified. "It's the first time I'm *glad* your sister's such a stick-in-the-mud," Lila said. "When do you think she'll return it—"

Lila's words were interrupted by the crackle of the school's PA system. A young male voice called for attention over the loudspeaker.

"Is that Winston?" Jessica asked as everybody in the hall stopped to listen. It wasn't the normal time of day for announcements—those were usually given in the first ten minutes of homeroom. And why was Winston giving the announcements?

"Shhh," Lila ordered. "It might be about the prom."

"I'd like to take this opportunity to read something very special to you," Winston's voice boomed through the halls. "I did not write this, but I think you'll enjoy it." He cleared his throat, and the

106

loudspeaker momentarily hissed with static. "'*Bruce Patman,*'" Winston intoned. "'Tall, with dark hair and blue eyes. Hot tennis player's body. Best feature: rich. Worst feature: kisses like a live jellyfish. Key word: *arrogant . . .*'"

Jessica's mouth dropped open, and when she glanced at Lila, she saw that her best friend's face had gone white. "Somebody will stop him," she gasped at Lila. "Right?"

But to Jessica's horror, Winston continued to read. The halls were filled with catcalls and laughter as Jessica and Lila stood frozen side by side, gaping at the loudspeaker over their heads. With every passing moment Jessica hoped that Sweet Valley would be hit by a giant earthquake. She'd prefer to be swallowed up in a huge crevasse rather than stand in the hallway and listen to her private opinions broadcast all over the school. But the names and descriptions kept coming until Jessica was blushing from head to toe.

Winston paused about a third of the way through the list. "I don't have time to read all of these," his thin, reedy voice called through the loudspeaker. "But I've taken the liberty of typing up this list. I'm sure everyone will want one of the photocopies I've made—free of charge, on a first-come, first-served basis."

"We're doomed," Lila moaned.

"That rat!" Jessica hissed. But then she realized something. Winston said he'd typed up the list!

"Hang on," she told Lila, trying to put a brave face on the disaster. "Nobody knows we wrote these. Everyone will think it's a joke—Winston's reading it, after all."

Then the PA system crackled to life again. "In case you're wondering—and I'm sure you are—the authors of this wonderful document are Jessica Wakefield and Lila Fowler," Winston announced cheerfully. "I have the original in their handwriting on file if anyone feels the need to see proof."

"We're doomed," Jessica agreed.

"No, wait!" Winston protested over the loud-speaker. "I was just trying to—" There was a sound of muffled argument, followed by a loud squawk as Winston was forcibly pulled off the air.

"At least he got into trouble," Lila observed grimly.

Jessica nervously peered down the hallway. All the other students were staring at her and Lila with shocked expressions. Jessica closed her eyes as she heard nasty laughter float down the hall. *This is bad,* she realized as the first blast of shock wore off. *This is very, very bad.*

"Not as much trouble as *we're* in, Li," she told her friend as they backed up against their lockers. "I don't think we've *ever* been in trouble like this before."

"Jess, I'm scared," Lila whimpered.

"So am I," Jessica replied.

But below Jessica's fear of what the guys were

going to do to her, another, darker emotion was simmering up.

Fury.

Jessica clenched her hands into fists. There was only one way Winston could have gotten his hands on that list.

How could Elizabeth do this to me? Jessica thought, fuming with anger.

Her twin was going to pay.

"I just don't know what to do about Blubber," Enid told Elizabeth, Olivia, and Maria Slater in the cafeteria at lunchtime. "Why is a big football jock interested in me anyway? Do I really look that desperate? I can't sleep because I'm up worrying about what I'm going to say to him if he asks me to the prom."

Elizabeth was shocked. She had no idea that Enid's problems with Tad had progressed this far! "First of all, you don't look desperate," Elizabeth said firmly.

"And second," Maria added, waving a carrot stick in the air, "if he asks you, you'll find a way to let him down gently. I know you will. You're very tactful. You can handle it."

"I told her that," Elizabeth agreed.

Olivia shoved her tray aside and leaned forward with her elbows on the lunch table. "Don't worry about it until he asks you," she advised Enid. "Why worry about something that hasn't even happened yet? Stay in the moment and deal with it when—*if*—it comes up."

"That's all good advice," Enid agreed miserably, toying with the straw poking out of her pint of skim milk. "But trying to *stop* worrying isn't the easiest thing to do in the world."

"Speaking of worrying, what about you, Liz?" Maria asked. "What's the story about you and *your* men troubles?"

Elizabeth sighed and threw half of an uneaten tuna fish sandwich back onto her lunch tray. "Todd and I were getting along great last night—we were working on setting up the country club ballroom," she explained to Maria. "But then Devon showed up."

"Ooh," Maria said.

"Exactly," Elizabeth concurred. "I mean, I was thrilled Devon was there, but I think I'm just getting friendly vibes from him too. I think he and Todd *both* just want to be friends now."

"The thing about vibes is," Olivia began, "it's all in how you interpret them. And Liz, maybe you're interpreting Devon and Todd's signals as friendly because you're too confused to handle anything else at the moment."

"Now I feel more bewildered," Elizabeth complained. "Don't confuse me, Liv."

"Sorry," Olivia replied with a laugh.

But suddenly Olivia's eyes grew wide, staring over Elizabeth's head. Beside her Maria sat up straight, looking concerned.

"What?" Elizabeth asked.

"Uh-oh," Maria told her. "Turn around."

Elizabeth turned her head and saw her twin barreling toward the table, Lila in tow. Jessica's face was twisted in a terrifying mask of anger, and she pushed aside anyone who dared stand in her path.

"Yikes," Enid said. "I wouldn't want *that* coming at me, that's for sure."

"Hurricane Jessica," Elizabeth muttered. She braced herself for her sister's arrival.

Jessica started right in. "How could you do that to me?" she demanded, waggling her finger in Elizabeth's face, fury pouring off her in waves. "How could you give my list to that . . . that clown?"

"Wait a minute—" Enid began.

"What are you talking about, Jess? I'd never seen your list before in my life," Elizabeth replied evenly. "Winston's announcement this morning was the first I heard of it."

"You guys," Enid interjected. "Liz brought the notebook to the country club, and Winston found the list. It wasn't Liz's fault."

Jessica gasped, sputtering in rage.

"And we're supposed to believe you?" Lila asked nastily.

"Believe what you want," Elizabeth shot back. "It doesn't affect me at all."

"You're all liars!" Jessica thundered. "Lizzie, I'll

never be able to trust you after this. Never!"

Maria stood up, her eyes blazing. "Liz and Enid wouldn't lie," she told Jessica forcefully. "And if you and your partner in crime did make that list, well, let me be the first to tell you—you deserve everything you get. Because that list is disgusting."

"Good luck getting a date now," Enid piped up.

Jessica's face turned red and mottled with fury. Her whole body vibrated, her eyes bulging out of her head. Lila peered over Jessica's shaking shoulder, staring daggers at Elizabeth and her friends.

"I'm not enjoying this conversation," Elizabeth told her twin calmly. "And I don't much like being accused of things I know nothing about. So why don't you come back when you're feeling more sensible?"

"Gaak!" Jessica screamed. She seemed past the point of coherence.

Lila took a step away from Jessica and peered at her friend with an expression of alarm. "I'd better get her out of here before she explodes," Lila muttered. Then she turned to face Elizabeth again. "You're not off the hook, Elizabeth," she warned. "We still know you did it."

"Whatever," Elizabeth replied with a shrug.

Lila shot a poisonous glare at her, then led Jessica out of the cafeteria.

A long moment of silence followed Jessica and Lila's departure.

"Yow," Olivia said finally. "That was *intense*."

"Your twin's really lost it this time," Maria added, sitting down. "Poor thing. She looked like she'd gone around the bend."

"Snapped for sure," Enid put in.

Elizabeth only let out a long sigh. "I just feel bummed out," she told her friends. "I can't even find their mess funny, even though I know they deserve it. I'm too much of a mess myself, I guess. Now my love life's a disaster *and* my sister's steaming at me for no apparent reason. I don't think my life can get any worse."

"Yes, it can," Enid replied. "You could have my life. That would be worse."

"Enough!" Maria commanded. "I am entirely fed up with the two of you sliding constantly into depression. That's not the point of the prom, is it? I don't have a date either, but you don't see me getting all sad and weepy over it, do you? Well, do you?"

Elizabeth and Enid didn't reply for a long moment.

"No!" Olivia cheered belatedly.

Maria groaned. "Listen, I've decided that if someone asks me, I'll go. If not, I'm not going to worry about it. Man, look at the two of you, sitting there like you just heard your puppies were killed. It's pathetic."

"I know," Enid moaned.

"Tell me about it," Elizabeth replied.

"Well, I'm not going to take it." Maria stared at

Elizabeth and Enid across the table with a fierce gleam in her eyes. "I'm going to figure out something to cheer you two up. And I *will* if it kills me."

"Not a chance," Enid moped.

"It's hopeless," Elizabeth added.

Todd dribbled the basketball up to A.J. Morgan, who hunkered down in a ready position to try to block Todd's shot. Todd faked left but drove to the right when A.J. lunged for the ball. He scored easily on a layup.

A.J. ran to recover the ball as Todd panted for breath.

"At least I've been upgraded to a *live* jellyfish," Bruce called from the sidelines, where he was standing with Aaron and Ken. He flipped through the pages of the catalog. "And *I'm* arrogant? This list is the most arrogant thing I've ever seen in my life!"

"We really need to teach those girls a lesson," Aaron said. "They've totally stepped over the line this time."

"Out-of-bounds," Ken agreed, shaking his head. "Offsides."

Todd dropped down into a crouch as A.J. advanced toward the hoop with the ball, really putting on defensive pressure. Just at the moment A.J. tried to shoot the ball over Todd's head, Todd leaped into the air, swatting the ball over to the sidelines again.

"Hey, Morgan!" Bruce hollered. "Want to hear what they wrote about you?"

"Not really," A.J. replied as he hustled to retrieve the ball.

Todd shook his head, wiping sweat off his brow as Bruce began reading from Jessica and Lila's list against A.J.'s wishes.

"Really cute and sweet," Bruce read, putting on a fake high voice that Todd guessed was supposed to sound like Jessica. "But his skin's too pale—looks bleached!"

A.J. dropped the basketball, his mouth hanging open. The ball bounced off his foot and rolled into the bushes on the far end of the blacktop court. Todd hurried to fetch it.

"Looks *bleached?*" A.J. repeated, obviously shocked. "I look *bleached?*"

"Maybe it's time for a tan, Morgan," Todd called over as he fished through the bushes for the ball.

"I can't tan," A.J. replied. He looked worried and offended by the list's report. "I'm a redhead— I burn. Plus who wants skin cancer? Man, I always knew Jessica was wild, but this is out of control! Even for her."

"She and Lila have obviously gone insane," Bruce intoned with authority. "Of course it wasn't a long trip for them, but now they've unpacked their bags and settled in to stay."

"Definitely!" Aaron shouted. "It looks like

Wilkins here got the *right* Wakefield twin!"

Todd blanched and hugged the ball to his chest. He quickly looked down at his high-tops, his face starting to burn with embarrassment as the other guys fell quiet.

Aaron had made a terrible mistake. Todd didn't have Elizabeth. *Worst of all,* Todd thought, *the guys know it's eating me alive.* If there was anything worse than having your heart stepped on, it was everybody knowing you'd had your heart stepped on. His friends' sympathetic, pitying looks made Todd grind his teeth. He had an almost overwhelming urge to hit something—hard. Preferably Devon Whitelaw.

"Hey, sorry, man," Aaron apologized to Todd. "I didn't think. Sometimes it's hard to remember that you two broke up."

"That's cool," Todd muttered, shaking his head as the words *broke up* made his stomach ache with misery. "Don't worry about it."

Ken plopped down on the grass at the edge of the blacktop, stretching out with his legs in front of him. He leaned back on his elbows. "But you *are* going to the prom with Liz, right?" he asked Todd.

"Bleached," A.J. whispered to himself, obviously still lost in Jessica's insult.

Todd slammed the basketball down on the blacktop and caught it again. "Yes," he told Ken. *I will ask her,* he decided firmly. *That's all there is to it.* "Absolutely."

"Yeah," Bruce drawled. "You and Liz have been going together so long, it wouldn't even be a real Sweet Valley prom without you two there as a couple. It would be just wrong."

Todd nodded, turning toward the basket. *Bruce is right,* he told himself. *Liz and I belong together—at the prom and everywhere else. We, like, represent the words* boyfriend *and* girlfriend *at this school. It's Liz's responsibility to go with me. It's her duty to be head over heels in love with me!*

He dribbled slowly toward the basket. *To . . . to love me as much as I love her,* Todd continued thinking. *To stop pushing me away. And to stop seeing that total creep Whitelaw!*

Todd set up the ball and launched it toward the basket.

Like Liz is really going to say no if I ask her, he thought.

The ball hit the rim and bounced into the bushes again.

Maria Slater held open the prom issue of *Dazzle* magazine in front of Elizabeth and Enid's faces, gesturing her hand like a display model at a young woman on the page whose hair was swept up in a sophisticated hairstyle. "This is what we're trying next," Maria decided. "You ready, Enid?"

Enid cringed. They'd been in Maria's bedroom for several hours, with Maria attempting to *force* them into cheerfulness by making them try various hairstyles. They'd already done *big* prom hair, like in the Miss America pageants. "No, no," Enid protested. "My hair can't take it. It's all going to fall out!"

"Your hair's not going to fall out," Maria growled, waving her hairbrush threateningly. "I told you I was going to cheer you two up if it killed me, so we're doing this. Besides, you two need to get prepared just in case someone does ask either of you."

Enid had never seen this side of Maria before—her insane hairdresser side, probably left over from Maria's days as a child actress. Enid was feeling a little scared.

Glancing over at Elizabeth, Enid saw that she was staring at Maria with a similar expression of fear. Elizabeth's giant, stiff helmet of coifed hair looked like a nightmare from a bad 1950s TV show.

Maria crept toward Enid with a big can of Freezit hair spray in one hand and a teasing comb in the other hand.

"Stop!" Enid cried, standing up. "Really, just stop. I mean, what's the point of getting ready? Nobody's going to ask me anyway. Except Blubber—and that thought's too depressing to contemplate."

But Maria didn't stop her approach. Enid backed away from her advancing best friend until she was trapped in a corner between a window with sunny yellow curtains and Maria's computer desk. "No!" Enid cried, waving her hands in front of her face.

Maria raised the can of hair spray. "Admit it," Maria crowed. "If Blubber asks you to the prom, you're going to go with him!"

"No!" Enid shrieked again. "I won't." But then suddenly she felt as though all the air had been let out of her. She groaned and slumped down against the wall until she was sitting on the floor. "Yes," she whispered. "He's not my idea of a perfect date, but if he asks, I just know I'm not mean enough to turn him down. My only hope is that someone else will ask me first."

"I knew it!" Maria said triumphantly. "That's fine with me—and it just proves that you need to start trying different hairstyles."

"I think you've inhaled too much hair spray," Enid told Maria. "Anyway," she said, struck with a means of escape, "*Liz* wants to go first!"

"Huh?" Elizabeth replied, turning to face her friends. "What?" Enid saw Elizabeth's eyes suddenly flicker with comprehension—she'd been staring into space with a bummed-out expression the whole time Maria had been stalking Enid.

Maria wheeled around and began stomping deliberately toward Elizabeth, her finger ready on the trigger of the hair spray can.

Elizabeth didn't even crack a smile. She just grabbed a baseball cap that was lying beside her on the floor and pressed it onto her head, crushing her big hair. "Don't," she moaned. "There's really no point."

"OK," Maria said. "Then answer this question." She smiled at Elizabeth. "If Todd and Devon both asked you to the prom *at the same time,* whose invitation would you accept?"

Enid saw Elizabeth shiver. She stared at her expectantly as Elizabeth closed her eyes, deep in thought.

But just as Elizabeth had blinked and was about to reply Maria's bedroom door swung open, revealing Mrs. Slater standing in the doorway.

All three girls turned to look. Mrs. Slater was a tall, striking woman as beautiful as Maria but a little plumper. She was dressed in a carefully tailored salmon business suit. "Hi, girls," she said. "Enid, there's a phone call for you. Someone named Tad."

Maria flopped backward onto her bed, cackling. Both Enid and Elizabeth couldn't help laughing. "Oh, no!" Enid cried. "You know, I told him I was coming here as an excuse for not having to deal with him tonight. I had no idea he would actually call me here!" She shook her head, feeling ready to laugh hysterically and burst into tears at the same moment. "I'm being stalked by an obsessive possible prom date!" she moaned.

"We have the makings of a very creepy slasher movie here," Maria said, giggling. "Oh, wait. There are already dozens of prom slasher movies!"

"Girls," Mrs. Slater broke in. "I try to encourage all kinds of free expression, but . . . but I'm not sure I like what you've done to your hair."

Enid stared at Mrs. Slater for a moment, and then she fell onto her back, gasping in laughter. "My hair!" she cackled. "Oh, it's awful." Around her she heard Elizabeth and Maria laughing loudly.

"So what should I tell this Tad fellow?" Mrs. Slater asked calmly, obviously not getting the joke.

Enid sat up and wiped her eyes. "Tell him . . . tell him I moved to Alaska," she replied. "That should hold him for a few days."

Mrs. Slater rolled her eyes. "*Alaska,* sure," she responded sarcastically. "I'll just tell him you girls went out." With that Mrs. Slater withdrew, closing the door behind her.

Enid stared at Maria and Elizabeth, heaving for breath. She hadn't laughed like that in a long time. And it had felt great.

"Couldn't you hide from your prom date someplace sunnier?" Maria asked Enid with a smile. "Girl, it's *cold* in Alaska."

And then all three of them were howling with laughter again.

Chapter 10

"We're being *ignored*," Lila hissed in horror.

Across from her Jessica slumped dejectedly against the vinyl seat in a booth at the Dairi Burger. *This has never happened to us before,* Jessica thought in shocked amazement. *Sure, we've been hated—but never, never ignored!* Used to always being the center of attention, she didn't like this new sensation one bit.

Fighting the sick, nervous feeling in her stomach, Jessica sat up as straight as she could. "Nobody ignores Jessica Wakefield," she muttered darkly. "And I'm going to prove it."

"What are you going to do?" Lila asked in a whisper.

"Watch this." Jessica turned and scanned the crowd of familiar faces in the Dairi Burger, searching for a likely subject. She quickly spotted Peter

DeHaven on the other side of the restaurant. He was one of the top contenders on her list. Jessica slid out of the booth and sauntered across the busy floor over to him.

Peter barely glanced up when she arrived. That set Jessica's nerves on edge, but she was determined to overcome his distance. "Peter," she purred, resting her hand lightly on his bare arm. "Hi, handsome," she breathed, batting her eyelashes. She turned the full force of her smile on him—a smile few men alive could resist. *He's mine,* Jessica thought triumphantly as Peter slowly turned to face her.

But Peter only smirked at her and then started to walk away.

Jessica grabbed his arm, squeezing it hard. "Wait!" she pleaded, dropping all pretense at flirting. "Don't run away. I just want to talk to you."

Peter chuckled nastily. "Why would you want to talk to me when I'm so *cruel,* Jessica?" he asked, arching his eyebrows. "Isn't that what you wrote about me?"

Jessica gaped at him for a moment, unable to think of a reply. Then she closed her mouth abruptly, turned around, and slunk back to the booth, feeling absolutely mortified from her head to her toes.

"We're in trouble," she told Lila as she slid into her seat. "It's your turn."

Lila sighed and looked around the room, peering

at possible guys. "There's A.J.," she said. "I'm going to try him. He's always sweet, and you've already dated him, so he's a good bet."

"Good idea," Jessica replied. "If anyone will overlook Liz and Winston's prank, it's A.J."

After shakily climbing to her feet, Lila smoothed down the waist of her blouse and took a deep breath. Grimly she started walking toward A.J.'s table.

Jessica watched A.J. smile up at Lila as she neared him. *So far, so good,* Jessica thought.

"A.J., you big sweetie," Lila flirted shamelessly, ruffling A.J.'s thick red hair. "You're looking very well this evening."

A.J. grinned. "For someone who looks *bleached,* you mean?"

Lila recoiled, stung. "No, no," she protested. "We didn't mean—"

"Save it, Lila," A.J. said. He turned and tapped on the shoulder of Suzanne Hanlon, who happened to be sitting at the booth directly behind him.

Jessica flinched and covered her face with her hands. Lila *loathed* Suzanne and always said that the tall, willowy brunette was the most pretentious human being she'd ever met. And for Lila to even notice when someone else was being pretentious, Suzanne had to be way affected. Jessica really didn't want to watch what she had a feeling was coming next.

But like slowing down on the freeway to peek at the victims of a car accident, Jessica couldn't not look. She splayed her fingers and watched as Suzanne smiled at A.J., with Lila frozen in place behind them.

"Hey, Suzanne," A.J. said smoothly. "I've been meaning to ask you this for a while. I'd consider it an honor if you would come to the prom with me."

Suzanne laughed happily as Lila's brown eyes blazed. Jessica winced at her friend's expression. Lila looked like she wanted to die—or *kill* Suzanne and A.J.

"Oh, I'd love to," Suzanne told A.J. with a warm smile. "I was hoping you'd ask me."

Jessica glanced away from the happy couple, her stomach in knots, as Lila managed to pull herself together and head back over to her booth.

After Lila had sat down, it took a long moment before Jessica felt brave enough to meet her friend's gaze. Lila was staring straight ahead at nothing, her shoulders quaking slightly. She looked racked with disbelieving horror.

"Ouch," Jessica said softly.

At first Lila simply nodded, but then her eyes narrowed suddenly, filling with an icy glint. "This is all *your* fault, Wakefield," she accused, her voice sharp with bitterness. "If you hadn't thought up the idea of the catalog—"

"*Me?*" Jessica gasped. "It was your idea right from the beginning!"

Lila just squawked in displeasure and turned away, her arms folded tightly across her chest.

Jessica shook her head. *It doesn't matter,* she decided. *I'm not going to give up yet. Not while I'm still alive and beautiful!*

Right then Aaron Dallas walked into the Dairi Burger. Jessica smiled. *Aaron's always been a good guy,* she thought. *One more try.*

Before Aaron even had a chance to sit down, Jessica had bulldozed her way across the restaurant over to him. He took a step backward, obviously surprised by the forcefulness of her approach. *Forget subtlety,* Jessica thought. *This is war!*

"So, Aaron, have you decided who your lucky date will be for the prom?" Jessica asked point-blank. "Could it be . . . *me?*"

Aaron pretended to ponder the question. "It's not you," he replied. He sat down at a nearby table. "I'm too *cranky* for you, remember?"

"Oh, let's put that behind us," Jessica said, forcing out a laugh. "A silly mistake. You can't imagine—"

"Excuse me," a voice behind Jessica interrupted. Jessica cringed, immediately recognizing the voice. "Please stop harassing my prom date."

Jessica wheeled around to face Heather Mallone. *Oh, no!* Jessica thought. *Not her.* Heather was tall, blond, extremely beautiful, and incredibly self-possessed. She was the cocaptain of the cheerleading squad along with Jessica, and the two girls had been bitter rivals from the first day Heather had moved to town. *Anyone but her!*

Heather sat down on Aaron's lap, and he clinched his arms around her waist.

This is a nightmare, Jessica thought.

"You're right about one thing, Jessie," Heather said mockingly. "Aaron does have great legs. I'm so glad he asked me to the prom."

As Aaron kissed Heather's neck, Jessica spluttered in horror, feeling as if her head was going to explode.

This is the worst day of my entire life, Jessica realized, closing her eyes. *Shunned by the boys at Sweet Valley High.* She popped open her eyes and pushed blindly through the crowd back toward the booth where Lila waited.

The world is coming to an end.

"Here," Devon told Elizabeth, passing her another silver Mylar star he'd just cut out of the crescent moon. The giant, sweepingly curved moon was spread out on a long table in the home ec room. Elizabeth silently took the star Devon offered her. She laid it flat on the table in front of her and began applying glue for glitter.

A few minutes later, halfway through cutting out another star, Devon paused, and Elizabeth glanced at him. She watched as he put down the scissors and yawned, stretching with his arms thrown wide. A tantalizing glimpse of his flat stomach was revealed as his tight gray T-shirt rode up slightly.

Elizabeth blushed and quickly looked down at the star she was working on. She'd dribbled glue right off the edge of the star. Frowning, she busied herself wiping up the excess glue with a paper towel she kept nearby for just that purpose.

She felt overly warm as he cleared his throat and returned to cutting out the star. Tension hung thick in the air between them, but it certainly wasn't unpleasant. *Just working side by side with him is kind of turning me on,* she admitted to herself, trying not to blush again. *I couldn't have found a guy more suited to my tastes if I'd invented him myself.*

Elizabeth sighed. *Well, there is one other guy,* she conceded. She looked up furtively, staring at the door. Todd had said he was going to show up at the committee meeting, but so far there had been no sign of him. *I wonder where he is. When he says he's going to be someplace, he always keeps his word.*

Shaking her head, Elizabeth returned her attention to the star she was working on. But a few minutes later her mind started drifting again.

Devon's been wonderfully helpful all afternoon, she thought, *but it's so obvious that he only wants to be friends. Otherwise wouldn't he have asked me to the prom already? He certainly doesn't seem to be on the brink of popping that particular question!*

Elizabeth shifted uncomfortably in the hard wooden seat. *And Todd doesn't even bother showing up anymore,* she continued. *So . . . no Devon, no Todd. I guess I should start looking for somebody else to go with me to the prom.*

She stared blankly at the star in front of her. It didn't look quite right somehow. Elizabeth idly turned it ninety degrees and saw that one of its points was uneven.

"Pass me the scissors for a sec?" Elizabeth asked Devon. Her voice sounded abnormally loud in the weighty silence that had been gathering between them.

Devon handed her the scissors, finger holes first.

As Elizabeth trimmed the edge of the star's point she wondered how she could go about finding somebody completely new. It seemed impossible. Her mind was a total blank about other guys. She couldn't even picture anyone's face besides Devon's or Todd's.

Maybe I should peek at Jessica and Lila's catalog, she thought, only half joking with herself. She let out a tiny snort of amusement. *Maybe they had the right idea after all. It is very useful to have all the guys described in a list!*

Distracted, Elizabeth closed the scissors on the tip of her finger. "Ow!" she gasped. A bright bead of blood appeared on her fingertip and started dripping.

Instantly Devon had her hurt hand in his own. "That's a serious cut," he said, sounding alarmed. His eyes narrowed in worry as he stood up, gently pulling Elizabeth out of her chair. "C'mon," he urged. "We've got to go take care of that. It could get infected."

"I'm *fine*," Elizabeth protested. "It's nothing." But she allowed him to lead her out of the room. He grabbed a roll of masking tape from a table as they left.

Devon steered her down the hallway toward the bathrooms.

"It's not a big deal," Elizabeth said. "I'm OK, really."

"I just hate to see you hurt," Devon whispered. He stopped in front of the boys' bathroom. He turned to face her, and Elizabeth nearly gasped, surprised and touched. *He does care about me,* she thought wildly. *More than I ever imagined.*

Devon kicked open the swinging door of the boys' bathroom. "Anybody in there?" he hollered.

When he received no reply, Devon led Elizabeth into the bathroom and over to a row of sinks. He turned on a faucet and gently held Elizabeth's finger under the stream of water, cleansing it.

Elizabeth glanced around the bathroom, wrinkling her nose in distaste. *It's so gross in here,* she thought. *How can boys* live *like this?* A strange odor Elizabeth didn't want to think about wafted over, and she labored to breathe out of her mouth.

Strangely, though, even the gritty bathroom felt cozy and romantic—as long as Devon was with her.

Devon finished rinsing her finger and began wrapping it carefully, lovingly, with toilet paper. He sealed the makeshift bandage with the tape he'd brought.

"Thanks," Elizabeth told him, feeling flustered. She couldn't help being entirely aware that she was completely alone with him. "I'm OK now."

"Then let's get out of here," Devon said softly. He took her hand and guided her out into the hallway again.

When the bathroom door had swung shut behind them, Devon stopped suddenly and turned to gaze into her eyes. "Sorry I overreacted," he apologized. "But . . . really, Liz, anything that hurts you . . ."

Elizabeth swallowed nervously and felt her face getting warm. *He feels my pain too,* she realized. *We're that connected.* Devon was standing so close that she could smell his wonderful, indescribable scent. She could feel his heat radiating out of his body, caressing her like a warm, familiar blanket on a chilly night.

And her head swam with delirious happiness as he took the injured hand he held in his own and raised it to his lips for a gentle kiss.

Todd stepped inside Sweet Valley High, humming a happy little tune. He smiled as he glanced down at the bouquet of flowers he was holding in his arms—a beautiful mixture of red and white rosebuds. They were almost—but not quite—as lovely as the person for whom they were intended.

I hope Liz is still at the meeting, Todd thought, a crease of worry furrowing his brow. *What if she left?* He strode more quickly down the hallway.

He hadn't meant to be so late. After school he'd rushed to a nearby florist, but the shop had been crowded, and it had taken him much longer than he expected to pick out and purchase the perfect assortment of flowers.

Then he had sat for a while in his car in the school parking lot, suddenly realizing that he was terrified, trying to figure out the exact right words to ask Elizabeth to the prom.

Elizabeth, we were always meant to be together, he practiced as he headed toward the home ec room. *Will you go to the prom with me? No . . . Elizabeth, you are the light of my life. The prom would mean nothing without you at my side.*

He shook his head and tried again. *Liz, you and me. The prom. How about it?*

Todd groaned. That wasn't even close. *You've got to sweep her off her feet, Wilkins,* he warned himself. *Dazzle her, don't give her a chance to say no. Think . . . romance. Take her breath away.*

He stopped short before making the final turn down the hallway that led to the home ec room. Todd inhaled deeply, calming himself as he slowly let out his breath. He had to get this right. It would really be his only chance to ask her. If he didn't go through with it now, he knew all his courage would leave him, and he'd be too afraid to try again. And if she said no . . .

Todd started walking again grimly. He wouldn't allow himself to consider the possibility that she might refuse his invitation. He just couldn't.

Elizabeth Wakefield, he thought, *will you do me the honor of being my date on the most romantic night of our—*

He turned the corner and saw Devon and Elizabeth at the far end of the hall. Todd stopped in his tracks. They were standing way too close together. And Todd easily recognized Elizabeth's body language—her head tilted up, slightly cocked, to look into Devon's face; the way her shoulders were slightly hunched. He tightened his grip around the wrapped stems of the roses, a single thorn poking him in the palm.

Then Devon kissed Elizabeth's hand.

Todd felt like he'd been socked in the gut. He swayed on his feet. *No, Liz,* he thought uselessly. *That should be me kissing your hand. . . . It should always be me. . . .*

But then Todd pulled himself together, and a surge of pure anger coursed through his body. *I've been such a fool,* he attacked himself, clenching his teeth. *I was* practicing *how to express my love for her . . . and she's obviously already made her choice.*

Without even telling me. Just letting me dangle on the end of a fishhook. When was she going to tell me? After the prom? I'm always the last to know.

Todd turned around. Fury raging within him, his mind spinning with self-pity and terrible accusations, he stalked down the hallway the way he had come.

On his way out of Sweet Valley High he dumped the rosebuds unceremoniously into a trash can.

Chapter 11

"Hi," Maria said as Elizabeth climbed into the backseat of Maria's car on Saturday night. Elizabeth just sighed in reply and nodded hello to Enid in the passenger seat. Enid grimaced—obviously in a funk as deep as Elizabeth's. *Perfect*, Elizabeth thought grumpily. *Misery loves company. And man, am I miserable.*

With a low growl Maria slid the car into gear and pulled out of the Wakefield driveway. "This is going to be one fun evening," Maria said sarcastically.

"I shouldn't be here." Elizabeth groaned. "I'm *so* not in the mood to have a good time."

"Exactly," Enid agreed in a morose voice.

Maria slammed her hand on the steering wheel as she maneuvered her car down Calico Drive. "I don't want to hear it," she warned. "It's my personal responsibility to cheer you two up, so no gloominess allowed tonight. Understand?"

"Fat chance," Elizabeth muttered. She didn't see any way the thick fog of depression that had settled over her could ever be lifted.

"It's the end of the school year!" Maria cried. "Party time! We are going to have a really, really fun girls' night out tonight. And I will not tolerate any self-induced depression!"

"Mine's Blubber induced," Enid said.

Elizabeth wanted to smile at Enid's words, but she just couldn't muster up the energy to make her facial muscles obey her.

"No, it's not," Maria argued. "It's all you. You're just putting too much expectation on the prom." She glanced in her rearview mirror. "And you can wipe that self-pitying fish mouth off your face, Liz. The same goes for you."

"You don't understand," Elizabeth complained, crossing her arms. "Devon was totally romantic yesterday, but he didn't ask me anything! I must've misunderstood his signals somehow—in a total state of delusion, I guess. And I haven't even seen Todd in days—"

"Stop!" Maria cried. "I said I don't want to hear it! And no, I don't understand. What's the big deal? I don't have a date yet either, but you don't see me moping around, do you?"

"You're in denial," Enid said. "You're Cleopatra."

"I'm who? Cleopatra?" Maria demanded. "What's that supposed to mean?"

Elizabeth sighed. "Cleopatra was the queen of

the Nile," she explained in a bored voice. "*De Nile*. Denial. Get it?"

"Nothing ruins a joke faster than explaining it," Enid complained huffily.

"Well, at least you *made* a joke," Maria said lightly. "That's something even if it was a bad one."

Elizabeth fastened her seat belt as Maria steered the car onto the freeway.

"And I'm *not* in denial," Maria continued. "I'm perfectly aware of what I'm feeling. I'm planning on hanging around with my friends all night at the prom anyway, so what does it matter who my date is? Why can't I just have a good time with my friends? Why does the prom have to always focus on *romance?*"

"That's the way it is," Enid replied. "It's a *prom*, not a quilting bee. It's *supposed* to be romantic."

Elizabeth couldn't agree more. But it looked like her chances for a romantic prom were dwindling faster than the light from a distant star.

Maria held up her hands in exasperation and then quickly grabbed the steering wheel again. "The prom has to be romantic? Who made up *that* rule?" she asked. "I'm going to think of it as a way of summing up the school year, as an opportunity to have a good time with my friends before the summer starts. I'm certainly not going to put any heavy romantic expectations on it. Now, you guys tell me if *that* doesn't make sense."

Maria was right—even in her misery Elizabeth

agreed with her friend's logic. But logic had nothing to do with the sense of deep loss she felt when she thought of going to the prom without Devon or Todd.

"I said *tell* me," Maria insisted. "I wasn't being rhetorical!"

"I guess," Elizabeth agreed grudgingly.

"Yeah," Enid added. "Whatever."

"I don't believe you guys for a second," Maria said. "You're both *so* holding on to your romantic hopes." Then she shook her head. "OK, OK, *enough* about the stupid prom. Aren't either of you curious where we're going?"

Enid shrugged. "Where?"

"I'm taking the two of you to a movie," Maria replied. "It's a horror flick called *Scream, My Sisters.*"

"Yuck," Elizabeth said, wrinkling her nose. "What do we have to see that trash for? Let's go over to the Plaza Theater and catch a foreign art flick."

"That's exactly what we're *not* going to do," Maria told her. "Foreign art flick equals romance. Which is why we're going to see *Scream, My Sisters.* It's about a crazed sorority girl who tries to kill her sorority sisters. It's the most *un*-couple-oriented movie I could find. There are barely guys in it at all!"

A moment of silence filled the car. At first Elizabeth stubbornly refused to be swayed into a good mood by Maria's plan. She *hated* horror movies. But then she chuckled softly to herself. *If I can't feel good about the prom,* she thought, *I might as well enjoy the exact opposite. And what could be more different from the prom than a blood-and-gore spectacle?* The thought made her smile.

Maria glanced back at her and grinned. "Elizabeth Wakefield smiling," she said in a fake-amazed voice. "How about that? Maybe miracles *can* come true!"

Jessica was waiting stiffly on the couch in the Wakefield den for Elizabeth to come home. When she heard a car pulling into the driveway, she clenched her jaw. *I'm going to kill her,* she thought, strengthening her resolve. The guys had totally humiliated her and Lila at the Dairi Burger yesterday, and Jessica had decided that it was all Elizabeth's fault. *There must be revenge! She's dead.*

As soon as the front door opened, Jessica twisted in her seat to glare daggers at her twin. But she felt a little taken aback by how *happy* Elizabeth seemed—she didn't even notice Jessica's dark stare.

"I had a *great* time tonight," Elizabeth said enthusiastically. "A fabulous girls' night out."

"It's nice to know that's possible," Jessica growled. "Because I'm going to have many, *many* girls' nights out from now on! And that's *all* I'm

141

going to have—thanks to you!"

Elizabeth blinked. Then she quickly plopped down on the couch beside Jessica with a sigh. "I think I figured out what happened with the list," she said.

"I'm all ears," Jessica replied, still glaring at her sister. "You have ten seconds before I kill you."

"I was in a hurry to go to the country club ballroom," Elizabeth explained quickly. "And Winston would not stop honking his horn. But I needed something to write on, so I grabbed the nearest thing . . . which turned out to be your notebook. I guess Winston opened it later and found the list. I really didn't know anything about the catalog, Jess. I swear it."

"Is that supposed to make me feel better?" Jessica demanded. "My life is ruined!"

"No, I guess not," Elizabeth replied softly. "But this might—I don't have a date for the prom either."

Jessica smirked. "That doesn't help," she said, sitting up straight on the couch, her voice rising. "Why should it? If you hadn't stolen Devon from me in the first place, I'd know exactly who I was going to the prom with now! And then I wouldn't even have had to make the list!"

Elizabeth shook her head, sighing. "Nobody can steal Devon," she argued. "He does exactly as he pleases. And only as he pleases. Your predicament is all your own fault, Jess. You should have known that catalog was a terrible idea."

For a second Jessica felt suffused with rage. *My fault?* she thought hotly. *How is it my fault? Lila thought up the idea, and all I wanted to do was find a nice guy to bring to the prom. Why does that make me guilty? And then if Liz hadn't grabbed it and Winston hadn't found it, I'd be home free! All I wanted was an honest list—*

But then she remembered the angry looks on the guys' faces in the Dairi Burger. She'd hurt them badly by writing down her true opinions. But that hadn't been her intention at all!

What was it Lila had said? *Honesty has a way of going over like a lead balloon. . . .*

Jessica really should have known the list would only lead to disaster. *It is my fault,* she realized.

She burst into tears. "I didn't mean to hurt anybody," she wailed. "I didn't know the list would . . . backfire so horribly! Nobody else was supposed to ever see it but me and Lila!"

"Shhh," Elizabeth murmured, opening her arms for a hug. "It's OK."

Jessica sobbed onto her twin's shoulder. "You should have seen their faces, Lizzie," she said tearfully. "All the guys hated me. It was so awful!"

"I'm sorry it turned out so badly," Elizabeth soothed. "I know you didn't mean for them to get hurt."

Pulling away and wiping her eyes, Jessica shook her head vehemently. "I really didn't," she sniffled.

"I do have to admit something," Elizabeth said with a weak grin. "I understand your impulse in writing that list. In fact, I've even considered thumbing through it myself."

"Really?" Jessica asked.

"Really," Elizabeth confirmed.

Jessica wiped away the last of her tears. "Hey," she said, managing a little smile. "Let's have some ice cream and go sit by the pool."

"Good plan," Elizabeth replied. She stood up. "I'll go get the bowls."

A few minutes later the twins were side by side with their feet dangling in the crystal blue pool, bowls of rum raisin ice cream in their laps. "So now what do we do?" Jessica asked, licking her spoon. "Both of us are dateless for the prom."

"Hmmm," Elizabeth mused. "Maybe Penny had the right idea—advertising for a date."

Jessica laughed. "That's too icky to even consider," she said.

"Is it?" Elizabeth asked. "Penny found a really nice, cute guy through her ad, and he's taking her to the prom. And remember, she even found Neil through a personal ad way back when."

Maybe . . . , Jessica thought. *Nah. That's way too desperate.*

But the scheming wheels in her head were already turning.

It's really not that *bad an idea,* she considered. *What if I did find some great guy from another school? A guy hotter than anyone at SVH. Someone who will really blow everyone away— make them regret they ever scorned Jessica Wakefield . . .*

"Uh-oh," Elizabeth said in a worried voice. "I know that look. What are you up to?"

"Oh, nothing," Jessica replied sweetly. She stood up, planning to rush inside and call Lila immediately. "I just need some more ice cream!"

Todd lay flat on his bed, staring up at the ceiling. *My life is meaningless,* he thought.

He had been so sure he'd eventually ask Elizabeth to the prom—and so sure that she'd eventually go with him—that he hadn't even considered a backup plan. *Stupid, stupid, stupid.*

The scene between Elizabeth and Devon kept circling in his mind, tormenting him. *Elizabeth standing, staring at Devon with rapt attention . . . Devon raising her hand to kiss it . . .*

Every time he replayed the scene, his chest ached, and he wanted to curl up into a little ball and never move again. But he couldn't stop himself from returning to the sight of Devon's lips kissing Elizabeth's hand over and over again.

And I was just waiting around for her to give me a sign, he thought. *I'm the stupidest guy who ever lived.*

Todd sat up, spotted a basketball lying on the corner of his bed, grabbed it, and hugged it to his chest. *Fine*, he thought bitterly, anger growing within him, blanketing over his misery. *If Elizabeth wants to throw out all the history she shares with me to go with Devon to the prom, that's just fine. Good for her. She's made her decision.*

But Todd didn't have to take it lying down. He knew just what to do to get her attention, just what to do to hurt her.

He knew just who to ask to the prom.

Todd smiled. *When Liz sees my date, she'll know exactly what she's missing,* he thought acidly. *She'll be eaten up with jealousy.*

And she's sure to come running back to my arms.

Chapter 12

"But I don't *want* a new dress," Enid protested as Maria dragged her through the mall after school on Monday. "What's the point anyway? To impress *Blubber?* And I shouldn't even be here— I've got a prom committee meeting in an hour."

Maria groaned. "You need serious help," she told Enid. "It's not certain you're going with Blubber . . . and this is a chance for you to dress up in a cool formal dress. Don't do it for Blubber—or whoever your date turns out to be. Do it for yourself. Have some pride. Remember: Romance is not the most important thing in the world. Self-esteem has to come first!"

"Gosh," Enid replied sarcastically as she followed Maria into the department store attached to one end of the mall. "What daytime talk shows have you been watching? That's the biggest load of psychobabble I've heard in aeons."

"And yet all true," Maria shot back. "Now come on!" She grabbed Enid's hand and pulled her along into the store's Young Miss section.

As they made their way toward the prom dresses in the back Enid was surprised to see that a rather large crowd had gathered in the center of the section around a small, makeshift stage. She broke away from Maria and stepped in for a closer look.

"What's going on?" Enid asked a little girl by her side.

The girl, who must have been around nine years old and had blond hair styled in a pixie cut, smiled as she stood on her tiptoes to see the stage. "It's that talk show, *Frankly Speaking*," she replied excitedly. "And *Jeremy Frank* is up there right now. He's gorgeous. They're doing a special on prom fashions."

"*Showbiz*," Maria scoffed. "It's just publicity for the store—and Jeremy Frank gets to wander among his *adoring* fans."

Enid had heard Maria explain often enough that she'd had her fill of the showbiz life during her years as a child model and actress, and she'd washed her hands of that whole crazy world. It just hadn't held any glamour for her once she had found out what really went on behind the scenes—all the phony attitude and faux friends.

Most of it made Maria sick, but Enid still found it pretty exciting.

"C'mon," Maria said. "Ignore this circus. Let's go get you a dress."

"No, wait," Enid replied. "It's not every day I get to see a TV star. Let's check it out." She started pushing through the crowd, angling closer to the stage for a better look.

Besides, Enid thought, *this will postpone having to try on prom dresses.* If she managed to waste enough time watching the show, maybe she'd need to leave for the committee meeting before she had to sort through the dress racks at all!

Maria reluctantly followed along.

Enid immediately recognized Jeremy Frank onstage. He looked a little shorter than he did on TV, but he was still handsome, with dark brown hair. "I think he's cute," she whispered to Maria.

"He's fine," Maria muttered. "If you like Ken dolls."

Enid watched as Jeremy introduced a young female model. The model sashayed out from the wings and sauntered across the stage, posing for the crowd.

"Isn't Joanna lovely?" Jeremy asked the audience, winking one of his blue eyes. "She's wearing an amazing Bunny Lane original in ivory chiffon—and you just know she's going to break every boy's heart at the prom!"

As corny as the whole scene was, Enid found

herself getting drawn in. Joanna *did* look lovely in her prom dress—almost good enough for Enid to want to get a dress herself. Almost.

I'd think about it if there was a guy I wanted to knock dead, she told herself. *But I just can't get excited about dressing up when the only guy who will pay any attention at all is . . . Blubber.*

Then Enid heard Jeremy saying something about introducing "the hottest male model on the West Coast!"

And Maria gasped by her side.

Enid quickly peered up at the stage as *Tyler Becksmith* strode out! Enid had noticed him in dozens of magazines—Tyler was quickly becoming very famous. He had glossy dark brown skin, massively broad shoulders, incredibly sharp cheekbones, perfect white teeth, and dazzling green eyes. He wasn't really Enid's type, but as he modeled his tuxedo she could see that he looked even better in person than he did in his pictures.

"He's a babe," Enid told Maria.

But when Maria didn't reply, Enid glanced at her friend. Maria's eyes were glazed over and fixed on Tyler, and she had an expression on her face that Enid couldn't read. "What?" Enid asked.

"I know him," Maria replied.

"You know *Tyler Becksmith?*" Enid asked in wonder. "How?"

Maria shrugged. "Oh, we did a bunch of photo shoots together when I was modeling in New York. Look at him! That boy can *certainly* fill out a tux!"

"That he can," Enid agreed.

Maria stared at the stage thoughtfully. And to Enid's surprise, Tyler paused onstage and gazed out into the audience—directly meeting Maria's eyes! And he *smiled!*

Enid's mouth dropped open. "I think Tyler just smiled at you," she told Maria in awe. *"Tyler Becksmith just smiled at you!"*

"He did, didn't he?" Maria asked nonchalantly. Then she shook her head slowly, as though she'd made a decision. "OK," she murmured. "I'll do it."

"Do what?" Enid asked.

"C'mon," Maria said, starting to push through the crowd. "Follow me."

Enid hurried to trail after her friend. "Wait, Maria," she called. "Where are we going? What are you going to do?"

But Maria didn't pause to reply. She quickly headed over to the left side of the stage. Enid was barely able to keep up.

"Maria, slow down!" Enid called.

Maria stopped abruptly by a curtain that partitioned off the backstage area. Enid almost ran right into her—just as Tyler stepped out from behind the curtain. Enid's stomach dropped. Tyler was almost too good-looking to exist in reality. Suddenly feeling shy, she stepped behind Maria to partially hide herself.

"Tyler," Maria asked calmly, "what are you doing in Sweet Valley?"

Tyler broke out in a big grin. "Maria Slater," he said, sounding pleased. "I *thought* that was you." He took a step forward and enveloped her in a big hug. "It's been *years,* hasn't it? I'm in town for about a month, doing some shoots up and down the coast. My agent thought it was a good idea for me to get some TV exposure."

"Well, you're looking good," Maria told him easily. "Oh, I'm being rude. Let me introduce one of my best friends." She stepped aside, revealing Enid. "Tyler Becksmith," Maria introduced them, "meet Enid Rollins."

"Enid, a pleasure," Tyler said in a warm baritone. He stuck out his hand for Enid to shake.

His hand was warm and very dry, and his shake was firm. Tyler smiled at Enid so brightly that she didn't think she'd be able to blink for a week. But when he returned his attention to Maria, she didn't seem dazzled at all—just happy to see him.

Just then a plump assistant popped her head out from behind the curtain. "Tyler!" she called. "Three minutes! And you still have to change your tux!"

"I'll be right there!" Tyler replied. When the

woman retreated, Tyler turned to Maria. "Gotta run," he told her. "But it's so good to see you, Maria. Any chance of us hanging out while I'm in town?"

Oh, wow, Enid thought. *Did he really just ask to hang out with Maria? Wait until Liz hears about this!*

Maria simply chuckled. "That's what I wanted to talk to you about. I don't mean to keep you, but I was wondering if a *prom*—a real one—sounds like fun to you at all. My junior prom is coming up soon, and—"

Enid's eyes popped open wide. Had she really heard Maria correctly? Her friend was the bravest person on earth!

"I'd love to," Tyler accepted happily. "It'll be great to spend time with you, and honestly, Maria . . . I'd be psyched to do something that has nothing to do with showbiz."

Maria laughed. "It's still a grind, huh?" she asked. "Even with your star rising? I see you in *all* the magazines, Tyler."

"It's a living," he replied with a shrug. "You know how it is—"

"One minute, Tyler!" cried a frantic voice from behind the curtain. "Get your butt in here!"

Tyler Becksmith's butt, Enid thought in a daze.

"You heard the lady," Tyler told Maria rue-fully. He gave her a quick hug. "I'll call you," he promised. "Leave your number with one of the assistants, OK?"

"Will do," Maria answered. "You'd better go!"

Tyler ran off, slipping quickly behind the curtain.

Enid immediately pounced on Maria. "I can't believe it!" she shrieked. "You just asked Tyler Becksmith to the prom! You really did it! *And he said yes!*"

Maria raised her hands defensively. "Chill," she told Enid calmly, but Enid could tell she was incredibly pleased with herself. "We're old friends. We spent like *months* together just standing around and chatting, waiting for shoots to be set up—and we became friends out of sheer boredom. He's a good guy, and it's no big deal."

"No big deal!" Enid exclaimed. "You just got a prom date. With a supermodel!"

Maria shrugged and smiled. "Yep," she said. "I sure did. Now let's go find a dress for you. *You* still need to look good for the prom too, remember?"

Enid let her hands fall limply at her sides, and all her excitement quickly drained away. She didn't want to be reminded of her own prom situation. Because now it seemed much, much worse.

Her friend had just gotten a prom date with a supermodel.

And what did Enid have waiting for her?
Blubber.

❖　　❖　　❖

Elizabeth typed furiously on one of the *Oracle*'s computers. She'd been assigned an article on the PTA's new source of private funding, but she had to get it done *now,* or she'd be late for the prom committee meeting at Maria Santelli's house.

She finished the last sentence and scrolled up to the top to proofread it quickly.

It looks fine, she decided. *It's not going to win me the Pulitzer Prize, but it's short and to the point.*

Just as she had hit the command to send the article to the printer Jessica and Lila suddenly burst through the door.

"Lizzie, you've got to help me," Jessica cried. "Now!"

"OK," Elizabeth replied with a shrug. "What's this about?"

"Tell her, Jess," Lila instructed.

Jessica rolled her eyes at her friend. "Duh, I was just going to!"

"Somebody tell me," Elizabeth said.

"OK, I've got a great plan," Jessica began. "I'm going to—"

"Uh-oh," Elizabeth interrupted. "Every time you have a great plan, someone gets hurt."

"Not this time!" Jessica replied. "This one's foolproof. Lila and I are going to place personal ads for prom dates! Isn't that a wild idea?"

Elizabeth couldn't help grinning. "Sure is,

Jess," she said, amused. "However did you think of it?"

"That doesn't matter," Jessica answered quickly. "Liz, we need your help writing the ad."

Elizabeth sighed. "I don't know," she said. "I've got to rush over to Maria's for the prom committee meeting—"

"Nobody will get there on time," Jessica argued. "You know those things always start late."

"Besides," Lila added, "you're *required* to help us since it was your fault that Winston got ahold of the catalog in the first place."

"I guess you're right," Elizabeth replied.

Should I place an ad too? she wondered briefly. *Todd and Devon are never going to break their silence and ask me.* But then Elizabeth realized how stupid and weak that thought sounded. *Duh,* she berated herself. *Why are you leaving it up to them, waiting for one of them to make the first move?*

Why don't I just decide who I want to go with—and ask him?

She sighed. She knew why not. *Because it would be too hard to choose.*

"Hello?" Jessica called. "Liz! Where did *you* just go?"

Elizabeth blushed, shaking her head to clear her bewildering mixture of thoughts.

Jessica stamped her foot. "Pay *attention*, Liz," she demanded. "This is important!"

"OK, OK," Elizabeth murmured, finally coming completely out of her minor trance. "So . . . what do you want this ad to say?"

Jessica snatched the hard copy of the personal ad out of the printer the moment it had dropped free. She peered at it, feeling very satisfied.

Lila tried to read the ad over Jessica's shoulder, but Jessica turned, preventing her from seeing it. She wanted it all to herself first.

> Attention! Two stunningly beautiful, charming young women, fed up with their school, are seeking perfect prom dates. Applicants must look strikingly handsome in a tux. Gentlemen only. No flaws a plus. Rich a double plus. Deadline 3 P.M. Thursday. Fax application to—

Lila grabbed the ad out of Jessica's hands. "Quit hogging that, Wakefield," she muttered.

"Check your fax number," Jessica instructed. "I didn't get to see it."

"It's right," Lila grunted as she read. "I especially like the part about *rich* being a double plus. The whole ad looks good."

"*Good?*" Jessica exclaimed. "It's *perfect*. It's sure to snag us the hottest dates in California."

"So," Lila asked, "which school newspapers do we place it in?"

"You'd better hurry and decide," Elizabeth put in. "Most schools print their weekly papers on Tuesday, and they come out on Wednesday. So you'd better get it to them by tomorrow morning, first thing."

"Definitely Lovett Academy," Jessica said. "I just adore those private-school guys. Yummy. And . . . Bridgewater High, I guess. Lots of rich boys in Bridgewater."

"How about Big Mesa and Palisades?" Lila asked.

"Let's skip Big Mesa," Jessica decided. "No surprises there. We've already dated anybody cute in Big Mesa. As for Palisades . . ."

Jessica let her voice trail away. She still couldn't think about what had happened with Palisades High without feeling a sharp, sad pain in her chest. Christian Gorman had gone to Palisades, and she had loved him with all her heart. Jessica still had nightmares about his tragic death in a gang fight.

"No," Jessica said softly. "Not Palisades."

"Fine," Lila replied quickly. "San Pedro High? El Carro? Woodgrove High? Ramsbury? Tierra Verde?"

"Yes, yes, yes, yes, and yes," Jessica answered with a smile. "Why not hit them all? El Carro High especially." El Carro was known for pretty much excelling in *everything*—academics, sports, arts, you name it. Jessica knew they'd get cool guys from El Carro.

"That's plenty," Lila said. "Let's start faxing!"

"Uh," Elizabeth broke in. "If you two don't mind, I'm going to rush off to my meeting."

"See ya," Jessica called, already bending over the *Oracle* office's fax machine. She couldn't wait to meet her new date!

Jessica grinned as she fed the ad into the fax machine. *Eat your hearts out, men of Sweet Valley High!* she cheered silently. *Jessica Wakefield is now a free agent!*

Chapter 13

Devon gave up trying to figure out the prom's seating chart and tossed his pad of graph paper onto a card table in Maria Santelli's living room. He just couldn't concentrate.

Where is Elizabeth? he wondered for the hundredth time. *Why hasn't she shown up yet?* If it had been anybody else he was waiting for, Devon wouldn't have given the lateness another thought. But it wasn't just anybody. It was *Elizabeth*—a girl famous for her punctuality. Even so, he could understand if she was ten or fifteen minutes late. But he'd been waiting for *forty* minutes, and now every tick of the clock made his heart clench.

He stared at the empty doorway, hoping she would appear. *Why does she have to be late today?* he wondered impatiently, his hands gripping the edge of the card table. *Could she somehow have figured out that today is the day I was planning to ask her to the prom, and she decided not to show up?*

He had finally decided to ask her. She'd tormented his every waking thought—and his dreams—long enough. As much as he wanted to wait until she no longer needed her space, he couldn't take the constant stressing over whether or not Wilkins was going to get to her first.

And after all, Devon reminded himself, *the worst she can say is no.*

For a moment he allowed himself to dwell on what would happen if she really said no. His heart twisted in agony at the very thought, and a sick, uneasy feeling settled in his stomach. If she said no, the pain would be nearly unbearable.

But I have to try, he told himself. *If I don't ask, I'll never know—and somehow that's worse.*

He glanced up at the door again just in time to see Elizabeth step inside. He sighed with relief. Elizabeth quickly waved to Maria, and then she hurried into the living room and grabbed a seat beside her friend Enid.

There's no time like the present, Devon thought. He stood up and made his way over to Elizabeth. He almost turned around and went back to sit down before he reached her, but she glanced up and smiled warmly at him. That smile gave him the confidence to reach her side.

"Hi," Elizabeth said, gesturing for him to sit down. "I was just telling Enid about Jessica's latest crazy plan. My twin's the one who made me so late."

"You'll love this," Enid promised.

"What's up?" Devon replied.

"Well, ever since her list got read over the loud-speaker," Elizabeth explained, "all the boys at SVH have totally ostracized her—"

"For good reason," Enid added.

"But of course that leaves Jessica without a prom date," Elizabeth continued. "So she and Lila have decided to place ads at a couple of other high schools nearby—advertising for guys to take them to the prom!"

Devon shook his head in amazement. "Do you think guys will actually answer the ad?"

Elizabeth shrugged. "Who knows? Jessica's schemes usually either crash and burn or they work splendidly. There's never any middle ground. So her plan could very well give her exactly what she wants."

"Maybe I should try it," Enid said softly. "I can't do any worse than what's already lined up for me."

Elizabeth coughed, and she pointedly averted her gaze from Devon. "Maybe *I* should," she muttered. "Nobody else is asking me."

That was a big hint, Devon realized. *Now, Whitelaw,* he ordered himself. *Do it. Ask her!*

"Elizabeth . . . ," he began.

"Yes?" she asked, her eyes wide.

Devon gulped "I—"

163

He stopped his question, staring, puzzled, as Elizabeth's face suddenly went pale. *What did I do?* he wondered, his palms starting to sweat. *I haven't even asked her anything yet!*

But then he realized that Elizabeth wasn't even looking at him—she was staring in shock at something *behind* him. And Devon noticed that a weird hush had fallen over the room.

He quickly turned to glance over his shoulder. Todd Wilkins stood in the doorway, looking smug, guilty, and angry all at once—like someone who wasn't proud of what he had done but had made his choice and must defend it to the death. Todd had his arm around a drop-dead gorgeous girl.

The girl looked somewhat familiar to Devon. But he couldn't quite place her—

"Courtney," Elizabeth whispered in horror.

That was it! She was the same girl Todd had started seeing when Devon and Elizabeth had first starting dating. Courtney Kane. *That seems like such a long time ago,* Devon thought. *Well, it looks like Wilkins has a date for the prom!*

He felt immediately guilty for feeling pleased that his rival was out of the picture but then heard Elizabeth choke down a sob. Devon turned around to look at her. She seemed heartbroken, staring down at the tabletop, her shoulders shaking.

Devon's first impulse was to gather her in his arms and hold her until her misery subsided. He felt furious at Wilkins for hurting her so deeply.

But then like a slap to the face, he realized what the depth of her misery *meant*.

I'm such a fool, he told himself bitterly. *She would never be that upset if she saw* me *with another girl.* Devon winced and closed his eyes to shut out the vision of Elizabeth's torment—an agony based on jealousy over the guy she really loved.

Todd Wilkins was her first choice all along.

After making sure Elizabeth was going to be OK, Enid took advantage of the commotion following Todd and Courtney's entrance to slip out the back door of Maria Santelli's house.

Please, please don't let Blubber have seen me leave, she prayed as she stood on the low back porch.

The Santellis' back garden was lushly overgrown with small lemon trees and clinging vines inside a high, brown-stained wooden fence. Enid hurried down off the porch and into the foliage to sit on a picnic table.

There was no sign that anyone had followed her. Enid breathed a sigh of relief.

If I can just avoid him a while longer, maybe someone else will ask me—someone I like, she thought. *And then I'll have a good excuse to let Blubber down.*

But how much longer *could* she avoid him, really? She was already running out back doors to escape—not a good sign.

Is a dream prom really too much to ask for? she wondered. *Don't I deserve that kind of happiness?*

Enid had no good answer for that question, so she sat silently on the picnic table, her hands between her knees. Idly she wondered how long she'd have to sit out there. The meeting was almost over, but that didn't guarantee that Blubber wouldn't hang around afterward. . . .

I'll sit out here all night if I have to, Enid thought with determination. *Anything to avoid a scene with Blubber—*

The screen door opened with a squeak. Enid glanced up—and saw Blubber stepping out onto the back porch. He had a single pink rose gripped in his left hand, and he seemed more fidgety and nervous than ever.

Enid's heart pounded as she searched around her for an avenue of escape. But unless she simply bolted and tried to climb the fence, she was trapped.

Blubber climbed down off the porch and slowly approached her, holding the rose in the air like a hall pass. "Uh, hi, Enid," Blubber mumbled.

"Hi," she replied, shaking her head gently.

Blubber's forehead broke out in a sweat. "Uh . . . ," he began.

Oh, no, here it comes, Enid thought. She reconsidered the idea of trying to scramble over the fence.

But no, she couldn't possibly be that rude. It

166

would *kill* him—and she'd never be able to face herself later.

"*Willyougotothepromwithme?*" Blubber blurted in a rush.

Enid sat up straight on the picnic table. "*What?*" She had understood his question, even as garbled as it was. But she was trying to stall for time, trying to gather her courage to turn him down.

I will be strong enough to say no, Enid told herself firmly. *I'll say I'm waiting for Mr. Right, whoever he is. I'll just say no!*

Blubber took a deep breath. "Will you go to the prom with me?" he asked, managing to speak the words at a normal speed. Then he ducked his head, as though he was expecting Enid to hit him with a brick.

Enid closed her eyes. She just couldn't hurt his feelings—especially not when he was so obviously *expecting* her to crush him like a bug. "Yes," she told him miserably.

Blubber's mouth dropped open in surprise. But his look of surprise was quickly replaced by a huge grin. "Great!" he cheered. He handed her the pink rose and smiled shyly, plainly overjoyed.

Enid tried to smile, but somehow she just couldn't get the muscles of her face to obey her command.

So much for my dream prom, she thought with a sigh.

＊　　　＊　　　＊

Elizabeth climbed the stairs to her bedroom, trying to ignore the empty, sore spot in the center of her chest where her heart used to be.

As she headed down the upstairs hall she heard Jessica and Lila laughing in Jessica's room over the sound of blasting dance music. Elizabeth peered in through Jessica's open door.

Jessica and Lila were totally dressed up, with parts of other outfits strewn all over the room. Jessica was wearing a black linen pantsuit with a black jacket over an iridescent green shirt. Lila had outfitted herself in white vinyl pants with a shimmery silver shirt. The two girls were boogying on Jessica's bed.

"What are you two up to?" Elizabeth asked.

Jessica's face lit up when she saw her twin. "Lizzie! Lizzie!" she cried. "Come dance with us! We're celebrating our genius idea!"

"What genius idea is that?" Elizabeth had to shout to be heard over the blaring music.

"The prom date ad, of course," Jessica replied. She sat down hard on the bed. "We've been trying on outfits all afternoon, planning what we're going to wear for our *go see*."

"Go see?" Elizabeth asked in confusion.

"That's what modeling agencies call interviews for models," Lila replied haughtily. "Open casting calls and the like. It seemed appropriate."

"Oh," Elizabeth responded.

Jessica climbed to her feet again and posed on

top of the bed. "So what do you think of my out-fit?" she demanded. "Perfect for our go see, right?"

"You both look very nice," Elizabeth answered diplomatically. "But aren't you guys sort of jumping the gun? You haven't even gotten any applications yet. The ad hasn't even *run* yet."

"We don't care," Jessica said with a big smile. She began jumping on the bed. "Don't rain on our parade, baby! We're sure to get tons and tons of replies—all from the most gorgeous guys on earth!"

Elizabeth sighed. She felt far too bummed out over seeing Todd and Courtney to argue. She hastily retreated back into the hallway.

"Wakefield," Elizabeth heard Lila threaten Jessica. "Stop *jumping*. You're going to make me sick."

Elizabeth continued to her room, which at least was neat and tidy if not absolutely quiet—she could still hear Jessica's music through their adjoining bath-room. She plopped down face first onto her bed.

She'd never felt more jealous in her life. Todd had seemed so happy to have Courtney by his side. *He deserves happiness, I guess,* Elizabeth thought, her eyes starting to fill with tears. *I can't begrudge him that. But why does it have to be at my expense?*

And Devon still hadn't asked her to the prom—he obviously just wanted to be friends. She'd given him such a strong hint at the meeting, but he'd let the opportunity to ask her pass by.

For a brief moment Elizabeth considered calling

up her brother, Steven, and asking him to take her to the prom.

How pathetic would that be? Elizabeth reprimanded herself, turning her face into the pillow. *My older brother taking me to the prom. I'd be the charity case of the century.*

The doorbell rang, and Elizabeth groaned. She'd have to get it. Jessica and Lila certainly wouldn't—even if they could hear the doorbell over the music.

She climbed out of bed and trudged downstairs. Elizabeth pulled open the door to find Maria Slater standing on the doorstep, a big grin plastered on her face.

"Hi!" Maria chirped, enveloping Elizabeth in a hug. "I have the most wonderful news!"

"C'mon in," Elizabeth said, feeling a little ungrounded by her friend's uncharacteristic display of cheery enthusiasm. She plodded over to the couch and collapsed onto it.

"You'll never *believe* who I ran into today," Maria said. Her eyes twinkled as she began to chatter about some guy named Tyler from New York she'd bumped into at the mall and how she'd asked him to the prom. Elizabeth was finding it difficult to pay proper attention. Maria's wavelength was way too happy for Elizabeth to really connect to it at the moment.

Maria sat down next to Elizabeth and nudged her on the arm. "So," she asked, "aren't you excited for me?"

Elizabeth blinked at her. "What?" she asked.

Maria groaned, rubbing her hands over her face. "My new prom date!" she shouted. "Girl, have you heard *one word* I've said?"

"Oh, *the prom date,*" Elizabeth replied. "Sure, I'm listening. I'm excited if you're excited. Are you guys just friends . . . or something more?"

With a deep sigh Maria slumped into the soft couch. "I don't know," she answered. "I really did feel something special this afternoon—something I haven't felt in ages. Liz, you know how long I've been single. *Forever.*"

Elizabeth nodded.

"But he's a *model,*" Maria explained. "And you *know* I don't trust those showbiz types—they're all bad news." She smiled, looking up toward the ceiling. "But Tyler used to be different. I'm just wondering if he's changed at all. Anyway, his gorgeous green eyes were just so *sincere. . . .*"

Elizabeth tuned out again, unable to focus on Maria's words any longer.

She couldn't get a single image out of her mind. *Todd, with his arm around Courtney Kane.* That image blotted out all her other senses until she felt as though she was falling into an endless spiral of misery . . . and jealousy.

Todd and Courtney.

Todd and Courtney.

Todd and Courtney.

Chapter 14

Devon grunted as he pushed himself through another sit-up. His abdominal muscles were aching, but this was the best way he knew how to work out his frustrations—purging his unforgiving emotions with pure exercise. His bare back was getting a little scratched up against the rough blue carpeting on his bedroom floor, but Devon didn't let that stop him. He had *lots* of frustrations to work out.

All he could picture was the miserable expression on Elizabeth's face the moment she saw Todd enter Maria's house with Courtney on his arm. The way her eyes had widened in shock, the way all the blood had leached out of her cheeks. And the way *he* had felt when he realized that Elizabeth would rather be with Todd.

He poured all his energy into performing the sit-ups, grunting and groaning.

Maybe it was just the initial shock of seeing them together, Devon thought. *That's why Elizabeth reacted so strongly. It didn't necessarily mean that she was dying to be with Todd.*

He collapsed flat on his back on his bedroom carpet. *Oh, nice rationalization, Whitelaw,* he chided himself.

Devon took a deep breath and started doing his sit-ups again. He didn't want to get Elizabeth by default either, now that Todd was out of the way. *I want to be sure she wants to go with me when I ask her,* he told himself. *If I ask her. When I ask her.* He stopped mid-sit-up, shaking his head. *I have to believe she wants only me. It's just not worth it to me if she doesn't care about me the way I care about her.*

But how could he know for sure? He grabbed his bent knees and held on. *Maybe there's a way to test her. . . .*

Devon quickly devised a plan as he rubbed his chin against his bare knees. *First I'll ask Liz out on a romantic date,* he decided. *Someplace special. She'll know immediately it's because I want to ask her to the prom. But then . . .*

He let go of his knees and fell onto his back again, reaching out to toy with the edge of the dark blue comforter that was hanging off his bed. *But then I'll send her flowers with a note from Todd! And . . . what will the note say?*

Devon scratched his chest, contemplating his

next move as he lay on the carpet. *OK, OK, the note will* apologize *for bringing Courtney to the committee meeting—and say that Todd changed his mind; he doesn't want to take Courtney to the prom after all. He wants to take Liz. I'll make it as gooey as possible—just like Wilkins would really write it. He can't live without her, all that stuff.*

Devon smiled up at the ceiling as his devious plan took shape. *Of course,* he thought, *Todd's note will beg Liz to come see him—on the same night as my date with her. It's perfect.*

Her decision would prove to Devon once and for all exactly who she really loved.

Sure, it's a little manipulative, he admitted, panting as he cooled down from his workout. *But all's fair in love and war. And I have to know the truth!*

He flipped over, climbed to his feet, and headed toward his bathroom to take a shower.

"Can you *believe* how many applications we got?" Lila asked Jessica as the two girls took their positions behind a huge oak table in Mr. Fowler's enormous conference room in the east wing of Fowler Crest. She gestured to the wide array of faxed responses spread out on the table in front of them. "It's stunning. We're more popular than I ever imagined."

The go see was supposed to be starting any

minute, and Jessica squirmed with growing anticipation in her chair, unable to sit still. "Of *course* I can believe it," she replied. "Who in their right mind *wouldn't* want to escort us to the prom?"

"The boys at SVH *not* being in their right mind," Lila added.

"Precisely," Jessica said.

Lucinda, the Fowlers' maid, opened the heavy conference room doors and stuck her head inside. "Miss Lila," she said nervously, "there are boys all over the foyer. I'm afraid they're going to break something. You should start seeing them now."

"OK, Lucy," Lila replied. "Send them in one by one. And if you can, pick out cute ones to go first."

"Yes, Miss Lila." Lucinda paused a moment. "Does your father know about this?"

"Of course," Lila answered. "He's given it his full approval."

"OK," Lucinda said, backing out. "I'll send the first boy in."

"Is that true?" Jessica whispered to Lila when the door had shut again. "Did your father really give his approval?"

Lila snorted. "Hardly," she said with a laugh. "Daddy would *freak* if he knew I was using his conference room to interview dozens of guys. But he's in Mexico with Mother, and what they don't know won't hurt them."

The conference room door creaked open. "One at a time, one at a time," Jessica heard Lucinda scolding the guys. Jessica couldn't help letting out a little squeal of excitement.

In stepped a tall, dark, gorgeous hunk who simply took Jessica's breath away. He was wearing a formfitting red Polo shirt tucked neatly into faded blue jeans. *A little more preppy than I usually like,* Jessica decided, *but way hot nonetheless.*

The hunk stepped forward, extending his hand to Jessica and then to Lila for them to shake. "Hi," he said in a deep, sexy voice. "I'm Trevor. Trevor Scott. Good to meet you both."

"Hi, Trevor," Lila purred. She quickly found his application in her pile. "Why don't you tell us a little about yourself? I know you filled out this application, but I'd still like to hear what you have to say."

Trevor stuck his hands into his pockets and rocked back and forth on his heels.

Nervous, Jessica thought. *Minus ten points.*

"Well," Trevor began, "I'm from El Carro High, and I'm single. I broke up with my last girlfriend two months ago—a mutual thing."

A mutual thing. Jessica smiled. *That means he was dumped hard.*

"I'm a senior," Trevor continued, "and I'm planning to be premed when I go to college in the fall." He smiled, a touch too smugly for Jessica's tastes. "I got into Yale."

"Yale," Lila breathed. "What kind of doctor are you planning to be?"

177

"Cosmetic surgery," Trevor answered. "The wave of the future. Did you know that the percentage of people who are getting surgical makeovers is rising exponentially every year? There aren't enough doctors to keep up. I'm getting onto that money train as fast as I can."

Jessica cleared her throat. She'd love to listen to Trevor chat about himself all day, but she had to keep things moving along or they'd never get to see all the guys. "Thank you, Trevor," she told him. "We'll let you know."

Trevor nodded and started to head out of the conference room. But before he exited, he turned around. "Did I mention I'm a great kisser?" he asked.

I'll just bet you are, Jessica thought. "Thank you, Trevor," she said firmly. "We'll let you know."

"I liked him," Lila said after Trevor had shut the door behind him. "A Yalie doctor would be perfection."

"He left me cold," Jessica admitted. "He was absolutely a hunk—no question—but didn't he seem a bit sharky to you?"

"Slightly," Lila agreed. She wrote down on the top of Trevor's application *Hunky but sharky Yalie doctor-to-be.*

"Next!" Jessica called out to Lucinda.

The door opened, and horror personified stepped in.

Jessica gaped at the skinny, gawky guy standing

in front of her. He was wearing a shiny polyester retro-seventies suit with his black hair slicked back. His nose was way too big for his face, and he had no upper lip worth mentioning.

"Hey, there," the guy said smoothly. "I'm Bernard, your love machine. And I'm here to answer all your prayers, foxy mamas."

"*Thank* you," Lila said abruptly. "We have your application. We'll let you know. Please shut the door on your way out."

"But baby," the guy said in an oily voice, "you haven't even seen me dance!"

To Jessica's chagrin, Bernard started humming loudly and shimmying in the middle of the conference room. He looked like a string bean getting random electric shocks.

"*Thank you*. That will be all," Lila said again. "Please leave," she added hastily.

"I know we'll make magic together," Bernard told Lila as he headed toward the door. "I'm awaiting your call."

When the door swung shut behind Bernard, Jessica burst into laughter. "What was that?" she gasped.

"That was my disco nightmare," Lila replied. "The less said about Bernard, the better."

"Next!" Jessica called out.

This time when the door opened again and the newest guy entered, Jessica sat up and gave him her undivided attention. He was really cute. He wasn't overly muscular, but Jessica could tell he had a good, trim body under his slightly trendy collared shirt and loose black jeans. The guy had a friendly face and deep brown eyes that Jessica could easily imagine getting lost in.

"H-Hi, I'm Jordan," he introduced himself. He swallowed as he stood with his hands behind his back in front of the big table. "Sorry I'm so nervous," he apologized. "This isn't exactly a normal situation for me."

"No problem," Jessica replied—and she meant it. She'd been turned off by Trevor's nervousness, but Jordan's seemed kind of endearing.

"Hello," Lila said. "Why don't you tell us a little about yourself, Jordan?"

"Well, OK," he began. "Uh . . . I'm a junior at Lovett Academy, although I can't seem to be as driven as most of the people there. I mean, some of them just seem insane—doing nothing but studying night and day. That's just not me."

"What *is* you?" Jessica asked.

"I play a lot of soccer," Jordan replied, "but it's not like I live and breathe sports, you know? I don't really know what I want to do, like after college, but I'll probably be some sort of artist. I love art in any medium."

Jordan must have misread Jessica's expression as negative because he quickly clarified his words. "Don't get me wrong," he said, "I'm not one of those tortured artists. I think it's a waste of time to

180

go about moaning about your life. I try to have as much fun as possible."

"Artist, huh?" Lila asked. "What do you plan to do to support yourself?"

"I'm not sure," Jordan answered sincerely. "It doesn't really matter, though. My parents only care that I keep myself busy and give something back to the world. I never really have to work. My family's sort of . . . well-off."

"One last question," Jessica said, "and then we'll let you go." She wasn't surprised at all to feel a sharp pang of regret that Jordan would be leaving. She definitely wanted to learn more about him . . . and maybe kiss his full, sensuous lips. . . . "Uh," she asked. "Can you dance?"

He broke into a heartbreakingly beautiful smile. "I *love* to dance," he replied.

As Jessica watched Jordan leave the room she knew she'd found her guy—even though he was only the third one they'd interviewed. Just something about him tugged at her heart and told her that he was exactly the right choice.

Sometimes you just know, Jessica thought. *And I just know. Of course, we have to sit through the rest of the applicants for Lila's sake, but otherwise I'd be happy to stop right now.*

When they were alone again, Lila turned to Jessica with a swirling, swooning look in her eyes. "I want him," Lila said. "That's the one I want."

"*What?*" Jessica cried. "Him? He's *totally* not your type."

"Meaning *what*, Wakefield?" Lila asked dangerously. "Why not?"

"I just can't picture you two together," Jessica argued. "He seemed so down-to-earth, and you're . . . not."

"He seemed very refined to me." Lila sniffed. "Obviously used to the finer things in life. We'd get along great—I can just tell."

"I really don't think so," Jessica replied stubbornly. "I think you should forget about that one."

Lila's eyes narrowed suspiciously. "Oh . . . ," she said. "*You* want him, Jess. Don't you?"

"Of *course* I want him," Jessica snapped. "Can't you see he's perfect for me?"

Lila chuckled. "I can see that you're seriously deluded," she said. "You going with Jordan to the prom would be like eating sushi with a fork. Gauche."

"Gauche!" Jessica thundered. "He'd see right through your flimsy layer of pretension, Li," Jessica told her hotly. "That boy is *real*. And your servants have protected you from anything real your whole life!"

"If by real you mean *common*," Lila replied haughtily, "then you're very wrong, Wakefield. Because I've been hanging out with *you* for years!"

Jessica couldn't help cracking a smile. "Good one, Li," she complimented her friend.

"Thanks," Lila said.

Jessica sighed. "We don't have to fight, you know. There are *tons* of great guys waiting outside. We don't have to argue over *one* of them. We'll each just choose someone else and get over this silly struggle over Jordan. That way neither of us gets him, but we still get to go to the prom as friends—with great dates."

"Who aren't Jordan," Lila added.

But Jessica could tell that she was going to agree—all she needed was another push.

"Lila, he was only the third guy," Jessica reminded her. "What are the chances that he's the only perfect date in the group? None. And even if there's *nobody* as good as Jordan, wouldn't you rather go with your *second* favorite and have your best friend with you at the prom, not hating your guts?"

"I suppose," Lila conceded. "OK, I'll scratch Jordan off the list. But there better be a close second, Jess!"

"There will be," Jessica assured her, totally psyched that Lila had given in.

Because there was no way Jessica was giving Jordan up. *On the night of the prom, when she sees me walk in on Jordan's arm,* Jessica thought gleefully, *Lila is going to be green with envy!*

But now she still had to find someone for Lila to take.

"Next!" Jessica called out to Lucinda.

Chapter 15

"Good-bye," Elizabeth told Devon warmly. She listened on the phone until she heard him hang up on his end. Only then did she gently put the receiver back into its cradle.

She hugged herself, feeling deliciously pleased. Devon, thoughtful as always, had called simply to confirm their date for this evening. *I can't wait!* she cheered silently.

Elizabeth hopped off her bed and stood motionless for a moment in the middle of her room. Then she twirled wildly, her arms outstretched. *It's going to be a beautiful night!* she thought. *And I'm sure tonight's the night Devon's going to ask me to the prom!*

She plopped back down onto the bed, relief coursing through her body. Sure, she was shocked about Todd and Courtney . . . but she loved Devon too, definitely. Maybe this was meant to be. The prom could be the start of a whole new life for her, a new, happy beginning.

Oh, it's sad that Todd's a thing of the past, Elizabeth decided, *but there's no use crying over what's done and gone—not when the future looks so bright! From now on I'm going to concentrate solely on Devon Whitelaw. And put Todd Wilkins into a little drawer marked Memories.*

After all, Devon was the one obviously devoted to her. And Todd could keep his horrible Courtney Kane!

Elizabeth raised her legs, kicking into the air, unable to contain her joy.

She heard the doorbell ring downstairs but didn't move. *Jessica can get this one,* she thought. *It's her turn. And I'm too happy to move!*

A minute later she heard her twin bounding up the stairs. Jessica burst into Elizabeth's room, waving a huge bouquet of flowers. "Look what you got!" Jessica called, amazement shining in her eyes.

Oh, they must be from Devon, Elizabeth thought as she accepted the flowers from her sister. *They're so lovely.* The bouquet was made up of deep purple tulips surrounded by small yellow carnations. She breathed deep inside the paper wrapping around the flowers, transported by the heavenly smell. *Devon's so sweet.*

"Read the card, read the card," Jessica insisted, and Elizabeth dug around in the bouquet until she grasped a small square envelope in her fingers. She pulled it out and opened it.

As she read the card she gasped.

It wasn't from Devon at all.

Todd sent the flowers. He'd written an apology for wasting his time with Courtney—and he admitted that he'd only started dating Courtney to make her jealous. *I love you more than anything on earth,* the card said. *And any moment away from you isn't worth living.*

Underneath, Todd had written that he wanted to see her.

Tonight.

Lila drummed her fingers impatiently on the arm of her love seat as she waited for someone to pick up at the other end of the line. *C'mon,* she thought as she listened to the ringing. *I don't have all day.*

After the fifth ring Lila was ready to give up. But just as she pulled the phone away from her ear, she heard a voice. "Hello?"

Lila immediately sat up straight. "Hi," she said pleasantly. "May I please speak to Jordan?"

"Speaking," Jordan replied.

Lila felt a warm thrill run up her spine at the sound of his voice. Barely able to control a tremor from marring her *own* voice, she told him, "This is Lila Fowler. And I've got very good news for you."

"Yes?" Jordan asked. He sounded a little nervous.

"Do you remember me?" Lila replied. She was sure he did, but she wanted to hear his reaction to the question.

"Of course," he said with a chuckle. "You were the gorgeous brunette sitting behind the table, trying to scare the living daylights out of me. And you know what? You succeeded. I'm totally surprised you called."

"Good answer," Lila purred. "And believe it or not, you managed to beat out all the other applicants, and I'm happy to inform you that you won the coveted position of accompanying *me* to my junior prom."

For a moment Jordan didn't reply, and Lila worried that he didn't want to go with her. *Maybe he* was *interested in Jessica,* she thought. *Maybe—as irrational as it sounds—he didn't like* either *of us!*

"Cool!" Jordan said enthusiastically. "I can't wait!"

"Wonderful," Lila breathed, immensely relieved and happy. He did like her!

"So what do I do now?" Jordan asked. "Do I get to see you before the prom, or do I have to wait until then?"

Hmmm . . . , Lila thought. *It would be good to go on a few dates with him before the big night so we can get comfortable with each other.* Besides, she wouldn't mind spending time with him anyway. But there was one problem. If Jessica found out that Lila was bringing Jordan to the prom, she'd go ballistic. And it would ruin Lila's surprise. She so wanted to see Jessica's face when she showed up with the sexiest guy in California—just the guy Jessica herself had wanted!

"We'd better hold off until the prom," Lila told Jordan. "Logistics will be tricky to work out before then. But afterward, who knows?"

"OK, that's cool," Jordan replied. "Anything else I need to know before then?"

Lila considered his question. "No," she answered. "I don't think so. Well, my dress will probably be an almost black dark green, so you might want to plan accordingly."

"Got it," Jordan said. "Thanks a lot, Lila. I just know we're going to have a great time!"

"I think so too," Lila replied. "I think so too."

Lila smiled as she hung up the phone. *He's sweet,* she thought. *But more important, I'm going to have the most handsome, charming date at the prom!*

"Too bad, Jessica," Lila muttered as she crossed her legs on the love seat. "This will be the *last* time you try to tell me who to date!"

Jessica stared at the phone in her hand. She was just about to dial Jordan's number to tell him that he'd won a date with the most fabulous girl on earth . . . but then she decided that telling him over the phone would be tacky. She dropped the phone back on its hook.

It'll much cooler if I go over there and tell him in person, she thought. *Just like the Publishers Clearing House sweepstakes thing! Except instead of a million dollars he gets me!*

Which is a much better deal, Jessica reasoned as she dropped to her knees to search under her bed for her shoes.

Jessica couldn't wait to see Jordan's face when she showed up to remind him in person of what he'd won. *His jaw will drop, and maybe he'll blush slightly . . . but then he'll definitely get control of his surprise, and that's when the sheer happiness will kick in!*

She slid into the shoes she'd found under the bed and turned to inspect herself in her full-length mirror. *Not bad,* she decided, turning to admire her clingy jeans and her loose white linen shirt. The strappy heels she was wearing made her legs look longer than they really were and made her calf muscles bulge in a sleek, sexy line under the stretchy material of her jeans. *This should knock his socks off!*

Only a few minutes later Jessica was behind the wheel of her mother's car, heading for the address Jordan had scribbled down on his application. Jordan lived in Cedar Springs, about forty minutes up the coast from Sweet Valley, near Lovett Academy.

She sang loudly along with the radio as she drove, and she had reached his house before she knew it.

Jessica pulled into Jordan's driveway and hopped out of the car. She had to remind herself not to run as she approached the front door. Jordan's house was a *mansion,* three stories high with thick white pillars and surrounded by acres of well-manicured lawn.

She rang the doorbell and shuffled her feet impatiently as she waited for an answer.

Jordan opened the door—and he looked just as cute as she remembered.

Jessica flashed him her most charming smile. "You have been chosen to represent all the males of the human species as their perfect ambassador to escort Jessica Wakefield to the Sweet Valley High prom," she intoned solemnly, winking at him so he'd know she was joking. "Do you accept this challenge?"

"Hi, Jessica," Jordan said with a smile.

But Jessica didn't think he looked quite as psyched or honored as she expected him to look. In fact, behind his faltering smile he seemed confused . . . and kind of sick.

"Are you OK?" Jessica asked quickly.

Jordan opened his mouth to speak but apparently thought better of it because he clamped his mouth shut and shook his head.

"Do you want to go to my prom with me or not?" Jessica demanded. She was starting to feel awkward—he was making her nervous. And she *hated* feeling awkward.

Jordan glanced around wildly, as though seeking the answer somewhere out on the lawn or in the driveway. But he still didn't reply.

"Well?" Jessica asked, putting her hands on her hips. "What's the deal?"

With another failed smile attempt Jordan finally met her eyes. "Sure," he said quickly. "I'd love to go."

"Great!" Jessica told him. "We're going to be the coolest couple there!"

"Don't I know it," Jordan replied. "But Jessica—right now I have to go, OK? I don't mean to be rude or anything, but can we talk about the details later?"

"Sure," Jessica said, a little taken aback.

He smiled warmly. "Thanks," he said sincerely. And then he shut the door on her!

Well, that *was abrupt,* Jessica thought as she turned around and walked toward her mother's car. *Not exactly the response I was expecting.*

Jessica shrugged. *Hey, whatever,* she decided philosophically. *At least now I have a great-looking prom date to go along with all my other prom accessories!*

Chapter 16

Devon sat on his motorcycle, lurking in the shadows down the street from the Wakefields' house, watching and waiting from his unseen vantage point.

Elizabeth was pacing nervously on the front stoop of her house, all dolled up in a long white dress.

But who's she going to see? Devon asked himself. *Me or Todd? That's the real question.*

Elizabeth crossed her arms, staring out into the night.

What's she waiting for? Devon wondered. *Why doesn't she just get into the car and head out?*

He was answered a moment later when Jessica drove up the street and pulled their mother's station wagon into the driveway. Elizabeth rushed toward the car. Devon watched as Jessica climbed out of the car and the twins exchanged heated words for a moment. He couldn't hear what they were saying, but he assumed Elizabeth was chastising her twin for being late as usual.

Finally Jessica relinquished the keys into Elizabeth's hand. Elizabeth quickly got into the car and backed out of the driveway.

Devon waited until Jessica was safely inside before he started up his motorcycle to follow the wagon.

It's the moment of truth, he thought as he rode his bike. He kept the station wagon in view at all times, but he was careful not to get too close. If Elizabeth spotted him, he'd never find out what he wanted to know.

Now that his plan was in motion, Devon felt almost sick with anticipation. *It'll be better to know,* he reminded himself. *It'll be a* relief *to find out who she really loves.*

He wasn't sure if he really believed that, so he concentrated on staying on her tail.

Devon trailed the wagon to a gas station, where Elizabeth stopped to refuel.

Of course, he thought. *Jessica left the tank empty.*

He had to circle the block twice until Elizabeth started driving again. Devon followed her to the edge of the city limits. She could still go either way—toward the restaurant just out of town where she was supposed to meet Devon or to the beach, where "Todd" had asked her to come.

Devon held his breath when she reached an intersection at a red light. He waited a few cars behind her for the light to change. *If she turns left, it's me she loves,* he realized. *If she turns right, I've lost her to Wilkins.*

The light changed, and his stomach dropped as she turned right.

Swearing under his breath, Devon almost decided to just turn around and go home. But then he shook his head, heavy under his helmet. *I'm going to see this through to the end,* he thought grimly.

He trailed her all the way to the beach. She stopped the car in the beach's parking lot and climbed out. Devon killed his motorcycle's engine before she could hear the sound of him approaching. He hopped off and pushed the bike into the shadows without ever taking his eyes off Elizabeth, deciding to continue following her on foot.

As he neared he saw Elizabeth stepping onto the sand. She looked absolutely beautiful in the moonlight, the wavering reflection off the water playing over her elegant white dress.

She's all dressed up for Wilkins, not for me, Devon thought ruefully. Idly he wondered what was in the small package she was holding in her hand. *Probably some love token for Todd,* he realized with a sharp pang of jealousy.

Elizabeth shivered in the chill seaside air, glancing around. Devon kept to the shadows of the edges of the parking lot, never stopping watching her. He saw her check her watch many times.

Devon clenched his hands to fists. The original,

debilitating, numbing shock of her decision to meet Wilkins was wearing off—and stabbing agony and cold rage were surging forward to take its place.

This is a betrayal, he thought icily. *And I'll never forget it.*

Elizabeth stared out at the dark waves lapping invisibly on the shore. She checked her watch again—she'd been waiting for over half an hour.

With a groan of exasperation Elizabeth wheeled around and stomped back toward the station wagon. *I give up,* she thought. *I can't believe I came all the way out here because Todd asked me and then he didn't even have the decency to show up.*

Elizabeth shook her head. *And I didn't even want to see him!* She had only come out to the beach to return the engagement ring he'd given her.

I should've called him after getting the bouquet and told him I was through with him over the phone, she chided herself. *I could've returned the ring Monday at school.*

She strode across the parking lot. *But no,* she thought. *No, I have to be nice. I wanted to spare his feelings by telling him how I felt in person.* So she'd trekked all the way out here—making herself late for her date with Devon. And he'd totally stood her up—leaving her on a deserted beach on a cool, windy night.

Elizabeth stared up at the crescent moon high overhead. She sighed. *Todd must be losing it,* she decided. *Being rude like this isn't like him at all.*

Elizabeth wondered if she really knew who he was anymore. She wouldn't have thought that parading Courtney around just to hurt her was like Todd either, but he'd done just that!

How could he expect a tiny little apology on a minuscule card to make up for how much he hurt me by seeing Courtney? she wondered, starting to become angry. *Did he really expect me to come running, ready to forgive him?*

She froze, tense as a wire, as she felt the floodgates of fury burst inside her. *This is the last time Elizabeth Wakefield is putting up with his selfish games!*

Elizabeth shook her head again and strode over to the station wagon, seething.

But as she opened the driver's-side door a movement caught her attention out of the corner of her eye. Somebody was stepping out of the shadows at the edge of the parking lot.

"Todd?" Elizabeth called out. "Todd, is that you?"

But as the approaching figure moved into the moonlight Elizabeth gasped.

It was Devon.

And his eyes glittered in the darkness like diamonds—sharp, hard, and as cold as ice.

Will Elizabeth and Jessica clear up their date disasters in time for the prom? Find out in Sweet Valley High #142, **The Big Night**—*the second book in a fabulous, four-part prom miniseries.*

Ask your bookseller for the books you have missed

You'll always remember your first love.

Love Stories

Looking for signs he's ready to fall in love? Want the guy's point of view? Then you should check out the *Love Stories* series. Romantic stories that tell it like it is— why he doesn't call, how to ask him out, when to say good-bye.